THEY CAME TO SANTA FE

Clay Reiner—His career as a troubleshooter was just a buildup to his most challenging stage run ever.

Beth Hanlon—Caught between the man she is planning to marry and the man to whom she is increasingly drawn, she must rely on her own inner strength to survive the journey.

Frank Colby—On the run from two secret crimes, he was a desperate man willing to trap his unsuspecting fiancé in his bloody plan for escape—and endanger every passenger bound for Santa Fe.

Amelia Winfield—Her love for her husband led her bravely toward a dangerously remote outpost, but she knew she could not help her bitter son learn the meaning of courage.

The Stagecoach Series
Ask your bookseller for the books you have missed

STAGECOACH STATION 6:
SANTA FE

Hank Mitchum

™ **BCI** Created by the producers of
**Wagons West, Children of the Lion,
Saga of the Southwest,** and
The Kent Family Chronicles Series.
Executive Producer: Lyle Kenyon Engel

BANTAM BOOKS
TORONTO · NEW YORK · LONDON · SYDNEY

STAGECOACH STATION 6: SANTE FE

*A Bantam Book / published by arrangement with
Book Creations, Inc.*

Bantam edition / June 1983

*Produced by Book Creations, Inc.
Executive Producer: Lyle Kenyon Engel.*

ISBN 0-553-23314-9

Published simultaneously in the United States and Canada

PRINTED IN THE UNITED STATES OF AMERICA

O   0 9 8 7 6 5 4 3 2

STAGECOACH STATION 6:

SANTA FE

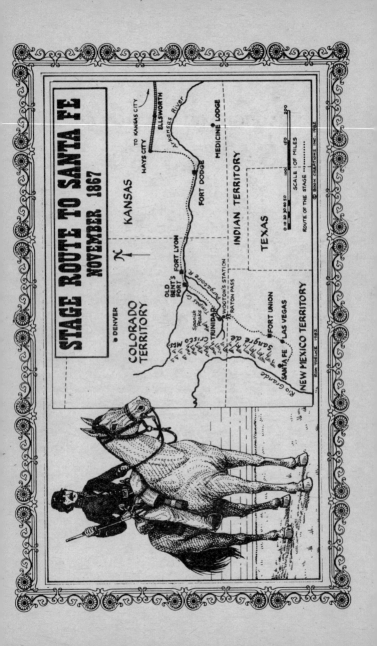

Chapter 1

Frank Darby scowled irritably, but in that ancient street, too narrow for more than a single footpath along one side, he could only draw back and place his shoulders against an adobe wall to make way for the approaching wagon. The Mexican driver, wearing a steeple hat that seemed to rest upon his shoulders, plodded alongside his slow-moving oxen and didn't give the gringo so much as a glance. One huge disk wheel almost rubbed against Darby as the dung cart groaned past, its ungreased axle squealing like a soul in torment.

Afterward, striding on and angrily brushing at the shoulders of his fine box coat, Darby silently cursed the man, the sullen day, the fiery native cooking that could corrode the gut, and this whole godforsaken pueblo, with its smells of dung and ancient dust. At the next intersection a gust of wind caught him without warning, whipping at his hat brim and raising a glittering film of grit that stung his eyes.

The wind's chill breath reminded him that it was November already. November 1867—and winter about to close in across the territory of New Mexico. One more winter to be trapped in this miserable pueblo of Santa Fe, this relic of a dead past with no living present and no immediate promise of escape to civilization!

Darby's mood was a poor one when he reached the house that was his destination. He savagely pulled the bell cord at a massive wooden door that was set into a blank

1

adobe wall, flush with the narrow street. But as the door opened, the scowl vanished from his smooth-shaven features, and he nodded and smiled at the old woman who looked out at him.

"Ah—Serafina! Good afternoon. I do trust you're well. And how's old Tom doing?" he added when that got no answer. "He's expecting me—the hotel had word for me to drop by."

He got no response at all from those sharp black eyes, which regarded him with open hostility. He had an uncomfortable feeling the old bitch could look right through him, with nothing but contempt for what she found behind the facade he carefully presented to the world. Now, without so much as a word, she pulled the door wider and grudgingly stood aside to let him enter. He shrugged, and went in past her.

Tom Hanlon's home was comfortably furnished, with heavy furniture of local manufacture and with things brought by wagon freight all the miles of the Santa Fe Trail. The living room, with its low ceiling and native stone fireplace where a piñon log burned, would always be cool in summer and warm in winter. A Navajo rug on one adobe wall gave the room a splash of color—reds, browns, and yellows.

As Serafina closed the big door, shutting out the chill of afternoon, Darby removed his hat. He indicated the hallway leading to the back part of the house. "I'll just go on back," he said.

The woman's black eyes merely returned his look with a cold stare, giving him nothing. Frank Darby nodded to her and smiled again, though he was sure Serafina knew well enough that the dislike between them was mutual. What bothered him most was the knowledge that, although he usually could mold other people's reactions in any way he pleased, here was one person he would never be able to fool.

He was well acquainted with the layout of Tom Hanlon's sprawling, one-story residence. Almost daily during these last weeks since his boss's accident—except for the past few days when business called him seventy miles away to the even tinier New Mexico pueblo of Las Vegas— Darby had traveled down the hallway to the room where Tom spent most of his time ensconced in a large bed that was slung by straps fashioned from the leather thorough-braces of a Concord stagecoach.

Entering now, Darby found the owner of the Hanlon Stage Line in his nightshirt, propped up against pillows with a lamp on the bedside table lighted against the deep-ening gloom of the clouded day. The bed was strewn with an untidy clutter of papers and correspondence. Some familiar-looking business ledgers were stacked beside the lamp—Darby recognized them and a frown involuntarily darkened his brow. He quickly smoothed it away as he approached the bed, saying heartily, "Well, Tom! You're looking fine! You're going to be up and out of that bed in no time at all."

Hanlon gave a snort. "I doubt I'm looking *that* good!" Weeks of pain had aged him, so that his cheeks appeared sunken and the great beak of a nose was more hawklike and prominent than ever. He looked suddenly two de-cades older than his fifty-odd years, but the gray eyes beneath their bushy brows were as fierce and alive as ever. He said heavily, "Doc's the same as told me I ain't likely to ever walk again." He scowled at his useless legs, stretched out beneath the covers. "I mean to prove him a liar. But it's gonna take a damn long time—and all the guts I got in me!"

"You'll make it," Darby assured him blandly. "There's no way they can hope to keep *you* down—not even by running a stagecoach over you!"

The older man lifted a shoulder impatiently. "We'll see. . . ."

Darby looked around, found a straight chair, and pulled it over by the bed. He seated himself and smoothed a palm over his thick and wiry blond hair. "I just got in an hour ago from settling that little matter over in Las Vegas. I found word for me at the hotel that you wanted to see me. Business, I take it?"

"That's right—business." But having said it, Hanlon seemed in no hurry to proceed. He studied the younger man, his brows knotted in a deep frown. The fingers of one hand silently drummed the bedclothes—fingers toughened by years of handling a freighter's jerk line or the leather reins of a four-horse stagecoach string. Abruptly then, he demanded, "Frank, just how long has it been since I brought you here to manage things at this end of the stage line?"

Not hiding his puzzlement at the question, Darby answered promptly. "Why, you know the answer to that. It's been just short of a year now."

"I been paying you well?"

"You haven't heard me complain."

"And for these past several months you been engaged to my daughter. . . ." The stern lips pursed beneath Hanlon's grizzled sweep of mustache. "That's why I got to ask you: Just what the hell do you think you been up to?"

Darby blinked. "Why, doing my job, I hope! Part of yours, too, since you've been laid up—such as running over to look into that situation at Las Vegas. I do believe I handled that well enough. Otherwise, I must say I haven't the slightest idea what you might be talking about!"

"Don't you?" Hanlon's mouth and eyes were suddenly hard, and a finger stabbed at Darby. "Look sharp, mister! I ain't much for bookwork, but I do know how to read a balance sheet and even track my way through a ledger. And that's exactly what I been doing this past couple of days while you been gone." He indicated the stack of books on the table beside him. "I asked Ned Archer to bring these over from your office, so I could have a go at them."

Ice was beginning to gather behind Frank Darby's

stare, but he managed to maintain a casual tone. "Were you looking for anything in particular?"

"I sure as hell wasn't looking for what I found! I was only trying to keep myself from going crazy while lying here wondering if I'd ever get out in the field again. I guess it's been a failing of mine that I could never bring myself to care enough about money. I run my business and leave them kind of details for someone else to see to. That's what I been paying you for. Hadn't been for this accident, no telling when I'd have found out what a damn poor job you been doing!" As he talked, he had been sorting through the papers scattered on the bed. He found one on which he had scrawled some figures. "Here! The best I been able to figure, this is a tally of the amount you been taking out of the company while nobody was watching!"

Darby only stared at the paper for a moment. Finally he accepted it and examined the figures it contained. The older man asked impatiently, "Well? You got anything to say?"

"Nothing—except that you've obviously misread the record."

Tom Hanlon stiffened. The anger he had been nursing boiled over. "Don't try to give me that, mister! Maybe I ain't never seen the inside of one of them colleges, but it don't make me stupid! At least I know stagecoaching, backwards and forwards. What's more, I carry a pretty good set of books right here in my head! I sure can tell when I see outlandish charge-offs for feed and equipment and business losses, and receipts that are way below what I damn well know they really come to!"

"You sound almost as though you're calling me a thief!"

"That's one word for it," the stage-line owner agreed crisply. "The law's got another one: *embezzler!*" And when the other man only returned his look, showing no outward reaction, Hanlon exclaimed, "Maybe you think I can't *prove* any of this—that I can't haul you into court?"

Frank Darby's manner was as cool as before. "Perhaps you could," he admitted, calmly enough. "But I doubt that you will."

"And just why the hell not?" Then Hanlon must have gotten his meaning, for the fire visibly went out of him. His shoulders dropped back against the pillows, and he glared at the younger man from under lowered brows as he answered his own question in a heavy voice: "Because of Beth! You figure I can't afford to see her get hurt by this!" And as Darby showed him the slightest of smiles, Hanlon swore fiercely. "Dammit! I shouldn't blame a young female for being fooled and not seeing through you—I never had the wits to do it, my own self! I only thank God that if this had to happen, it came at a time when she's back there in Missouri visiting her ma. She won't ever need to know how you went and made fools of us both!"

"You have something in mind?" Darby suggested mildly.

Apparently he had come to a conclusion. "I'm willing to make a deal with you," Hanlon said bluntly. "For *her* sake—and to get this damn thing settled and done with! No telling how much you may have stole from me altogether. I ain't sure I even want to know! I'll settle for what's wrote on that paper. Give me that much back and we'll call it quits. I'll let you off—without prosecution."

He may have thought the other man would jump at such an offer, but Darby was in no hurry to agree. He only lifted an eyebrow as he continued to study Hanlon coolly.

"I don't see that I'd be getting a great deal out of this."

"Oh, don't you?" Hanlon snapped. "Ain't it enough, for one thing, that you won't have to go to prison—or see yourself nailed with the name of an embezzler? The only condition I'm making is that you leave Santa Fe and agree never to see my daughter again."

"Suppose *she* doesn't agree?"

"Are you serious? Beth is a sensible girl. I'll do all I can to spare her feelings, but she'll hear enough that it ain't likely she'll ever want another thing to do with you!"

"I wouldn't be too sure about that," Darby warned smoothly. "She's pretty keen on me. Let's just suppose you're wrong, and that she's still going to want to marry me. Will you promise not to stand in the way?"

"*Promise?*" Fury almost tore a scream from the old man, and quite likely he would have bounded from the bed if a pair of smashed legs hadn't held him back. "I don't have to promise you a thing, you sonofabitch! By God, if you don't beat anything I ever seen, for gall and for—for slick, smooth-faced—"

He broke off, sputtering and incoherent, and fell back helpless against the pillows. At the same moment, the heavy tread of the housekeeper sounded in the hallway— her employer's furious shouts must have reached Serafina and brought her to investigate, anxious for his well-being. Waddling into the bedroom, she cried out in voluble Spanish, demanding to know if the señor was in pain, if he needed her, if she should send for the doctor. . . .

Old Tom Hanlon impatiently waved her away. The rush of angry color faded, leaving his sunken cheeks ashen and his lips trembling. But if his strength was shaken, his smoldering stare remained as furious as ever. After the woman withdrew with a suspicious and baleful glance at Frank Darby, the invalid seemed able at last to trust himself to speak.

"Beth can be pretty damn self-willed," he said in a voice that had fallen to an angry rumble. "Like me, I guess. If she decides she still wants you, even after all this, then maybe there ain't really much I can do about it. But I'm counting on her to show better sense. And meanwhile, getting back to what I said before, I want that money you took. Otherwise you can damn well face the consequences!"

Darby considered this a moment in silence, teetering

on the back legs of his chair while he measured the strengths and the danger of the crippled man on the bed. Presently he decided on his answer.

"I can't blame you for thinking this all looks very bad, but as for stealing—I flatly deny it! I was just trying to make some money for the company." He chose to ignore his employer's scornful snort. "The point is, I saw the chance for a good investment in mining stocks with a Denver company. That's where the money went. You never took any interest in company finances, and I wanted to prove that your faith in your business manager—your future son-in-law—was well founded. Now, if you'd just be willing to wait a bit, until the deal pays out—"

"No chance!" the older man exclaimed. "I *won't* wait—and I won't let you put me off with any drummed-up excuses!"

"Oh?" Darby shrugged. "Very well. It means I'll have to make a trip to Denver and see about liquidating my holdings. I can be ready to leave on the morning stage. You'll have to allow me a couple of weeks before you turn the wolves loose on me."

Hanlon shook his head. "I'll let you have *one* week. Not a day more! If you put any value on your hide, you'll be back by then—with the money. You get my meaning?"

"Perfectly!" For the first time, the sting of the old man's tongue-lashing had pierced Darby's cool composure. He felt the warmth of the blood that crept into his cheeks. On his feet now, he returned Hanlon's stare for a moment longer. After that, convinced of the futility of argument, he tossed the incriminating sheet of figures onto the bed. Then he turned abruptly on his heel, drew on his hat, and strode from the room without another word.

In three brief days away from the office, work had stacked up—but Darby gave no thought to it now. Instead he went to the Exchange Hotel—a new name for the establishment known as La Fonda, which from the start had served as an end-of-the-trail mecca for traders and wagonmen of the Santa Fe Trail. He had a room there, dingy and shabbily furnished by his standards, but he had put up with it for almost a year. The window looked out on the wind-whipped plaza, with its dusty trees and, on the north, the arcaded front of the old Governor's Palace. Still seething from the encounter with his employer, Frank Darby stood at the window and stared, unseeing, as lamplight began to glow in the windows of ancient adobes.

His earlier sour reaction to the thought of another winter in this baked-mud sprawl of a village came back to him now, increased tenfold by the scene with the boss of the Hanlon Stage Line. He had no doubt that the old man meant just what he said, and that he would carry out his threat to prosecute. It made no difference that Darby had put nearly a year into running the Santa Fe office efficiently and smoothly, while Tom Hanlon spent his own days in the field running hither and yon like a small boy with a stage line for a plaything. If the missing funds weren't returned within the specified week, it was clear Hanlon would move heaven and earth to put Frank Darby in prison.

What the old man didn't know was that there wasn't any money, in Denver or anywhere else. That mining property had turned out to be a rathole, swallowing up the good money Darby threw into it in a futile and frantic attempt to recoup his original lost investment. Everything he had taken from the company funds—every cent of it—was gone, except for a mere thousand dollars of his personal savings, which lay stashed away in a drawer of the old dresser that stood in a corner of the room. Nothing else was left—there was no way at all he could hope to raise the amount Hanlon insisted on.

As he turned from the window, Darby's busy brain was already circling, hunting a way out of his problem. He crossed to the table, dug up a match, and lighted the oil lamp against the settling gloom of darkness. As the flame

9

caught and steadied, its glow touched the photograph of Beth Hanlon that she had given him just before leaving last summer on a visit to her mother, who lived in a small town outside Kansas City, Missouri. Darby took up the photograph and examined the sunny features and the level gaze of her soft-gray eyes.

That lovely face, with its bewitching smile, had worked a magic on Darby almost from their first meeting. Beth Hanlon was an obsession that had gotten into his blood, different from any of the women he had casually known and discarded. At times he thought he could almost hate her for the way she had upset the timetable of his ambitions, which always had been focused squarely on himself. Infatuated nonetheless, he had brought all his charm to bear in a campaign to sweep Tom Hanlon's young and rather unsophisticated daughter off her feet. And by the time she had left for Missouri, she was wearing Frank Darby's ring on her finger.

His mouth hardened now as he spoke into the silence: "All right, Hanlon—you bastard! You think you can take her away from me? You're never going to get the chance!"

As quickly as that, his plans were made. He was ready for action.

Darby slipped the photograph into a pocket of his coat, and there discovered a letter to Beth, still unfinished, that he had been working on. He opened it and glanced through it, then without hesitation ripped the pages in two and dropped them into a wastebasket. No need to finish it, now that all the circumstances had changed. Whatever he had to tell the young woman would be conveyed to her in person.

A carpetbag sat on the bed, where he had dropped it on returning an hour ago from his business trip to Las Vegas. Darby crossed to a dresser, began pulling out the drawers, and tossed additional items onto the bed. Finally, he took from the bottom drawer a canvas money belt and a metal box. He opened the box and began to fill the canvas pouches with gold coins and greenbacks from his cache—all he had left in the world.

He was smiling tightly as his fingers worked, quickly and efficiently. Frank Darby traveled light, and he was ready for the road. If Santa Fe and Tom Hanlon expected to see him again after stage time tomorrow morning, they would have a long wait coming!

Chapter 2

In Hays City, Kansas, the cloud ceiling dropped a steady, icy drizzle that helped hold back the daylight. Though it was almost eight in the morning on this Wednesday in November, the Kansas plains seemed to lie under the faint glow of earliest dawn. Lamplight bloomed yellow in the windows of the city, pierced by streaking rain that flattened plumes of smoke above the town's chimneys. In front of the office of the Hanlon Stage Line, the light gleamed wetly on a coach made up and preparing to roll, its four-horse string stomping restlessly under the needling of windblown rain.

Sam Gaines, a dour and seasoned stage driver, moved around and fussed over his harness, swearing at the chill stiffness of the leather. Clay Reiner, chief field agent for the Hanlon Stage, came along the sodden sidewalk with a pleasant greeting, which he didn't expect would receive a reply—he knew the driver's moods and respected them. Gaines would thaw out later, but at this hour of the morning it was best to leave him alone. Reiner paused a moment to inspect the coach and team, with an expert eye that found everything in order for the four-and-a-half-day run that lay ahead.

The local agent, a man named Pete Kelland, came from the station weighted down with luggage. He set down his burdens and prepared to stow them in the rear boot under its leather cover.

"We all set to roll, Pete?" Reiner asked.

"Still shy a passenger," the man said as he worked at weather-stiffened lashings. "He hasn't shown up."

"It's practically time to roll."

Sam Gaines, hearing this exchange, paused in his inspection while he spat into the mud at his feet. "The sonofabitch! It don't matter to some that we got a schedule to keep! We ought to go without him."

To a veteran stage driver like Sam, passengers as a breed were simply a nuisance meant to make his job more exasperating. Knowing this, the stage companies put another man on their coaches for runs like this one to Santa Fe that covered far distances and many days of steady travel. Called a messenger or conductor, he bore full authority and responsibility for the stage, and for its passengers and whatever else it carried. Drivers were changed at frequent intervals, but the conductor remained on the stagecoach for the full length of the trip. Even the most seasoned and arrogant of reinsmen had ultimately to take his orders.

It was as a conductor on Tom Hanlon's coaches that Clay Reiner had made his mark after being invalided out of the Union army back in 1862, when a sniper's bullet at Shiloh had spared his life but left him with a shoulder that even yet would stiffen up in wet weather such as this. Recovered but restless, he had drifted west and found work with Hanlon, quickly rising to his present post of troubleshooter and general agent for the hundreds of miles of stage trace following the old Santa Fe Trail across the plains to New Mexico Territory. As chief field agent, he was directly responsible to Hanlon for the smooth operation of the entire line.

"You be ready to roll," he told Sam Gaines. "I'll worry about the customers."

Reiner turned toward the entrance of the stage office, where the buttery glow of oil lanterns inside the building combated the damp and gloomy morning. As he approached,

14

the door opened suddenly, and someone stood silhouetted in the light.

"Clay?"

The voice that spoke his name was one that quickened his pulse. And as he answered and moved toward her, Beth Hanlon stepped out and closed the door behind her. They stood enveloped by the drumming of the rain on the wooden awning just above their heads.

"It's so good to see you!" she exclaimed, and impulsively laid a hand on his sleeve under the poncho. Reiner was pleased to notice that she was warmly and sensibly dressed—for this weather and for the journey ahead. She wore a heavy coat and a fur cap that framed a heart-shaped face, turned a rosy color by the chill. Her eyes were a soft gray, and a fringe of brown curls showed beneath the edge of the cap. She was not a tall woman, and she had to lift her head to meet his gaze.

"Seemed like you were gone a lot longer than six months," he said grinning. "Was it a good visit?"

"It was fine. That is, until—" Her own smile was replaced by a quick, serious look. "Oh, Clay! I've been waiting for the chance to hear just what *you* know about Pa!"

He matched her change of mood. "I'm afraid it's not much more than was in that wire I sent your mother. I keep getting reports out of Santa Fe with almost every stage that comes through. But there really isn't much that's new."

"Exactly what did happen?" And as he hesitated: "I want to know all of it, Clay. You don't have to hide anything from me."

"I know that," Reiner said, and meant it. "My understanding is it was a freak kind of accident—in the hills somewhere south of Raton Pass. According to the man who was driving, the horses spooked at a mountain lion. Tom was standing in the box, trying for a rifle shot at it, and he got thrown off. The wheels caught him."

The hand on his arm tightened. "It's a wonder he wasn't killed!"

"Oh, I don't know." Clay tried to lighten his tone. "Tom's a little too tough for that."

They were interrupted as Pete Kelland headed for the station door, and they had to draw apart to let him enter. Afterward Beth persisted with her questioning. "How badly *was* he hurt? Please tell me the truth!"

"I can only tell you what the doctor's supposed to have said. I'm afraid Doc Griswold doesn't hold out too much hope that he'll ever be able to walk again. Still, you know Tom—he may fool us all."

Searching his face with a troubled look, she asked quietly, "Do *you* believe that?"

And Clay could only shake his head. "Not really, I guess." He added quickly, "But you understand, I haven't been to Santa Fe or seen your father since before the accident. I've had my hands too full with things here."

He knew he didn't have to go into details. Beth would understand what a busy time this had been for her father's chief field agent. With the Kansas Pacific Railroad building steadily toward Denver, the stage line's mail contract had required them, twice in the last half year, to shorten the route by moving their terminal to the new railhead—to Ellsworth in July and now, effective November first, still another fifty miles west to Hays City.

This latest shift had meant abandoning over one hundred fifty miles of established route, closing down stations and switching personnel and stock and equipment to a more direct line south from Hays City to Fort Dodge on the Arkansas River. As usual, there had been barely enough time for everything that needed doing—and Clay Reiner was the man who'd had to do it.

"So I haven't been able to talk to your pa myself," he concluded. "Maybe, in a way, it's just as well."

"How do you mean?" Beth wanted to know, puzzled.

"Simply that when Doc Griswold wrote me the news,

he said Tom had made him swear not to trouble you with it—he didn't want your visit spoiled. But you see, *I* hadn't made any such promise. And it seemed to me you'd feel worse if nobody told you. I knew how close you and Tom have always been. Anyway, that's why I took it upon myself to send the wire."

"Oh, and I'm glad you did! Believe me, Mother and I both appreciated it!"

"What about your mother? How has she taken all this?"

Beth shook her head. "The whole thing hit her pretty hard." She hesitated. "When she left Santa Fe for Missouri last year, she really meant it to be forever. She still loves Pa—I'm sure of that—and yet she felt, and still feels, there were reasons she just couldn't go on living with him any longer. Then this news came, and it truly upset her to think she wasn't on hand to help when she was needed. She decided at once, if there's anything at all she can do, her place is to be with him. And so we started west as quickly as we could. You did get the telegram that said we were on our way?"

Clay nodded. "There are places for you on this coach. You'll be leaving in a few minutes." Once again they had to make way for the agent, who came out between them with more freight to load.

A new thought seemed to be troubling Beth. Reiner sensed her faint hesitation before she asked, "That thing you said Pa made the doctor swear to . . . do you suppose he might have insisted on Frank making him the same promise?"

"Not to tell you? I wouldn't be at all surprised."

"I only wondered. . . . Though he's been writing every week I've been gone, he never once mentioned the accident—and I couldn't help wondering why. But what you've told me may explain it. Naturally, if Pa made him promise, Frank would never go back on his word."

"Naturally."

Reiner tried not to speak gruffly, but he couldn't help it if much of his pleasure at seeing Beth after so many months was suddenly dampened at mention of Frank Darby. Jealousy was not an emotion he liked to admit to, where Beth was concerned.

Angry at himself, he changed the subject. "I had business out of town till late yesterday. Soon as I got in I checked at the hotel and found out you'd already arrived on the train, but I figured it'd be better not to bother you then."

"You wouldn't have bothered us," she said quickly. "Naturally Mother and I have been anxious for the chance of a talk."

"The night clerk told me there was a man with you. Your uncle, he said."

"Yes. I think you've heard me speak of Uncle Harris. Harris McRae—he's in the mercantile business in Kansas City. When Mother and I decided on this trip, he tried at first to talk us out of it. He said it was too far to travel by stage—the two of us alone, and winter coming on. When that didn't work, he made up his mind to accompany us himself. Said that somebody responsible had to be along to take care of his sister and his niece, and to see that nothing happened to us."

"Oh?" Reiner didn't know whether to be amused or angry. "It doesn't sound as though he has much confidence in his brother-in-law's stage line."

"I'm afraid that's Uncle Harris," Beth said ruefully. "Perhaps you will understand when you meet him."

At that moment, a shift in air currents flung a sudden gust of wind at them, with needles of chill rain rattling against Reiner's poncho and causing Beth to duck her head. Reiner said tersely, "Your uncle could be right about one thing—this late in the year, you can see some bad weather between here and Santa Fe. It may be a rough trip." He took her elbow and turned her toward the door. "Let's go in—get you warmed up while you have the chance. . . ." He opened the door and ushered her inside, afterward closing the panel against the wet wind that pummeled the muddy street.

Like everything else in this hastily built end-of-track town, the stage-line office was crudely put together of unseasoned lumber that already was beginning to warp, so that the probing fingers of the wind had little trouble picking at the cracks and finding entry. A fire had been started in the iron stove, but it wasn't having much effect as yet. Tom Hanlon's wife, Mary, stood near the stove, warming her hands as she chatted with a woman and a half-grown boy who sat waiting on a bench against the wall. As the door opened, she turned around, smiling as she exclaimed, "Why, it's Mr. Reiner!" She seemed pleased to see him again, after a year and a half.

Greeting her, he removed his wide-brimmed hat and shook the rain from it. The woman continued, "Beth's been telling me about all that you've done for my husband while I was gone. She says you've made yourself invaluable."

"Oh, I don't know. I try to do what I'm paid for."

Voicing the matter that was uppermost with all of them just now, Beth said, "I was just asking Clay about Pa. There doesn't seem to be any new word."

"I'm afraid not," Reiner admitted. "At least he seems to be no worse, from such reports as I've been getting. He was pretty bad hurt, though a long way from being fatal."

"But—he's going to be crippled?"

He nodded. "From what I hear. I'm sorry." He added, "I know Tom's going to be glad to see you, Mrs. Hanlon."

"I hope so," she replied, but he thought she didn't sound too sure of it.

Clay looked at her, wondering about this woman who had left her husband without warning eighteen months before, and now—from feelings of guilt, her daughter said—was returning in the wake of his disastrous accident. Mary Hanlon had always seemed to him a handsome woman; after all, Beth's mother would have to be. At one time, she must have been beautiful. But her eyes were stained with shadow, and if she had ever shared Beth's sunny and outgoing nature, some discontent or disappointment must have subdued it—perhaps some flaw in her relationship with a man like rough Tom Hanlon.

"I've been so out of touch," Mary commented. "Is everything going well for the stage line? I mean, I hope Tom hasn't had business troubles, too."

"We seem to keep rolling," Reiner assured her.

"When I read in the newspaper that Wells Fargo had bought out Ben Holladay's Overland Stage, I couldn't help worrying what it would mean for Tom."

It struck Reiner that for a woman who had deserted her husband, she showed a revealing amount of interest in and concern for the way Tom Hanlon was faring.

"Wells Fargo has a lot more money than us," Reiner admitted. "But I can't see that they're going to be any real competition. They're completely tied up now with Holladay's northern route to California, along the Platte River and on through Salt Lake City. Our mail contracts to Santa Fe won't interest them."

Beth put in, "But what about the railroad? At the time Pa started his stage line, the stagecoaches rolled from Kansas City clear to New Mexico, and the trip took more than a week. Coming west this time, we rode the rail cars all the way here to Hays City—only four days and a half from Santa Fe. What's it going to do to us when the rails finally reach Denver?"

Clay smiled at her concern. "I wouldn't worry yet. There's the whole Southwest waiting to be opened up, and a southern route to Los Angeles. No, there'll be enough business to keep the Hanlon stages rolling for a good many years yet."

"I hope you're right," Mary said. "It would be a shame for the line to die—now—after all the sacrifices that have been made for it." And when she said that, he couldn't fail to hear an edge of bitterness in her words.

The agent, Kelland, came tramping in just then for a box that had been kept behind the counter. As they watched him carry it outside, Reiner felt a touch at his elbow. Turning, he saw the woman who had been seated with the boy on the wooden bench by the stove.

"Pardon me," she said. "Mr. Reiner, is it?"

"Correct. What can I do for you, ma'am?"

"I just wanted to know if I heard right. Is it four days and a half to Santa Fe?"

Reiner nodded. "That's what you heard. Barring mishaps, we'll be arriving there Sunday evening." She was a pretty woman, blond and brown-eyed, with something fragile about her that made him suggest, "I hope that's not too much traveling for you."

"Oh, I don't think so." And she smiled slightly, as though she read his thought and was amused by it. "After all, my son and I left Pennsylvania a little over three weeks ago. We've come by wagon and riverboat, and on the railroad cars from St. Louis. So I don't think we're worried about a few days in a stagecoach."

He couldn't help staring. Pennsylvania! Any idea of fragility must have been badly mistaken, and it immediately vanished in the tolerant humor of her smile.

"I'm not too afraid of the wild West, either," she said, showing him her reticule. "There's a little gun in here, which I carry for protection. So far I haven't had to use it once!" She added, "I'm Amelia Winfield, Mr. Reiner. This is Johnny."

Reiner had noticed the boy seated beside her on the wooden bench. Probably eleven or even a little older, he somewhat resembled his mother, but with a masculine cast to his features that would fill out from their present bony thinness. Now Amelia Winfield beckoned, and after a moment's reluctance, he lunged to his feet and came to take the hand Reiner offered.

"Hello, Johnny," Clay said, but got no answer. Though the boy stared directly at Reiner, he said nothing, and

Reiner didn't know if his frowning silence expressed moodiness or sullen hostility.

His mother went on with her explanation. "We're on our way to join my husband. He's a lieutenant in the army, stationed at Fort Union—that's near Santa Fe, I understand."

"About a hundred miles this side, which will cut a few hours off the trip for you," Reiner said.

"That will be nice," Amelia said. "It *has* been a long trip."

"Then I sure hope this last stretch goes well. For you too, Johnny," Reiner said, determined to get some kind of response from the youngster. But Johnny Winfield only looked at him passively before turning away.

Beth Hanlon had caught what Reiner had said, and asked, "You said *we'll* arrive Sunday evening. Does that mean you're going to be on this stage with us?"

"I didn't mention that? Yes, I am, as a matter of fact. For the past month I've been tied down here, switching the stage line to Hays City. Now I'm anxious to get out to Santa Fe, report to Tom, and see for myself just how he's doing. So I'm taking this stage through."

He didn't mention his strongest motive: This coach would be carrying a cargo that was doubly precious—Tom Hanlon's family, including the woman whom Clay Reiner, seeing her again after her long summer's absence, knew beyond a doubt he was hopelessly in love with. He knew he could entrust the safety of this particular run to no one else—even though, at their destination, he would be turning Beth over to the man she was engaged to marry. . . .

The street door opened again, and this time both Pete Kelland and Sam Gaines entered. Kelland looked around the group. "Well," he said. "The stage is ready to roll, but we still seem to be shy a passenger."

"And would you look at the time!" Sam nodded his shaggy head at the clock ticking on the wall. "I say it again—we ought to leave without him! Let him cool his heels a couple of days waiting for the next coach west. Teach him something, maybe."

Kelland consulted a paper he had taken from his pocket. "The name appears to be McRae."

"That's right," Mary Hanlon told him. "He's with us. Harris McRae—my brother."

"Oh?" Kelland's surprise showed in the way he blinked at her. He quickly recovered. "Of course, Mrs. Hanlon." And he turned hastily to Gaines, before the driver could start another angry protest. "Sam, you'll remember I told you—you're gonna have Tom Hanlon's family with you this trip."

The man was caught with his mouth already open. It took a moment for Kelland's meaning to sink in, and then Gaines's mouth snapped shut and his weathered features turned slowly red. Kelland finished lamely, "So naturally, we'll just have to wait for him."

"He still should have been here on time," Clay Reiner objected. He knew how his driver felt, and he shared the man's exasperation. "Do you have any idea what could be holding him up?" he asked Mary.

It was Beth who answered. "He was in his room when we left the hotel. I spoke to him through the door to remind him what time it was, and he assured me he'd be along directly. Said he had a letter he was writing."

"*A letter!*" Reiner felt a stirring of anger, and he heard Sam Gaines, unable to restrain himself, vent a disgusted snort. Reiner looked at the clock on the wall; its hands already pointed to ten minutes past the scheduled departure hour of eight.

Mary showed real distress. "Oh, I'm terribly sorry!" she exclaimed. "I can't imagine why he's so late. He knew perfectly well . . ."

Solid and deliberate footsteps sounded on the soaked planks of the sidewalk, approaching the stage office. Everyone looked toward the door as, without a sign of haste, the newcomer turned the knob and shoved it open.

Clay thought it would have been easy to identify Mary Hanlon's brother. There was a strong resemblance, but in Harris McRae the family's good looks had taken on a cast of smug self-satisfaction. He was a large man, clearly vain about his appearance, and putting on extra weight as he entered prosperous middle age. Now he seemed disgruntled over the rain that had partly soaked his clothing on his way from the hotel.

"This beastly weather!" he grumbled to no one in particular. He took off his derby hat and shook it, revealing a receding hairline above the smooth, clean-shaven features. "All I can say is, it's a foul time of year to be making a trip anywhere, for any reason!"

He seemed aware for the first time of the people silently staring at him. He frowned. "Is something wrong?" he demanded. "That coach out there *is* leaving for Santa Fe, isn't it?"

Sam Gaines shifted his boots. "Yeah," he grunted. "Finally!"

In a reproving tone, Mary Hanlon turned to her brother and said, "Really, Harris! Don't you see how late we are? And all because you had to write a letter! You shouldn't have to be reminded that it's important for a stage line to keep its schedule."

To that he only gave a negligent shrug. "Other things are important, too. Last night I remembered some instructions I failed to leave with that chief clerk of mine. It's imperative that he get them. I don't want him doing something stupid while I'm gone."

"But Henry Peterson is an intelligent man," Mary insisted. "There's no reason he can't be trusted to keep a store running on his own for a few weeks."

Her brother looked at her. "You think so? Believe me, I didn't become a successful merchant by putting that much confidence in a mere underling!"

Unable to keep silent, Reiner spoke sharply. "It seems to me, if you knew there was a letter that had to be written, you could have taken care of it last night. Why keep a whole stageload of people standing around waiting?"

McRae swung his head, and his cold blue eyes rested on the other man for a long moment. "I don't think I know you."

"The name is Clay Reiner."

"Oh, yes—I think I've heard it. You're an employee of my brother-in-law, right? Well, you can believe that I'll have something to say to him about the insolence of some of those on his payroll!"

Reiner heard Beth Hanlon's indrawn breath. He knew she was about to protest, but he didn't wait for it. "You do whatever you feel you have to," he suggested, meeting the man's look squarely. "And so will I. I don't know if you've traveled much by stagecoach, but the next four and a half days we're all going to be riding this one together. We'll stop only for meals. We'll be crowded, and I guarantee some of us will get on each other's nerves. Meanwhile, I'm responsible for the coach and the safety of everything and everyone on board. It's up to me to see that we get where we're going, when we're supposed to. There may be times when a quarter of an hour, like the one you've just lost us, is a lot more than an inconvenience—and if I can help it, that's not going to happen. Is that understood?"

"You've made yourself clear enough!" McRae snapped, his voice hot with temper.

"Good." Reiner turned away. He hadn't meant to speak up like that, but McRae had angered him. He wasn't surprised to see approval in Sam Gaines's grin. He even got a smile and a nod from Beth, which only served to remind him that this trip would end in delivering the girl he loved into the arms of Frank Darby.

Clay Reiner's manner was abrupt as he gestured toward the door and the stagecoach waiting in the rain. "Let's load up, then," he ordered. "Sam, fetch the mail sack. We were supposed to be on the road a quarter of an hour ago!"

*   *   *

At Hays City, Kansas, it had been raining this morning, but here in Santa Fe, four hundred miles away as the crow flies, the city basked in heatless sunlight. Santa Fe sat seven thousand feet high in the Sangre de Cristo Mountains, and the thin air at that altitude seemed to bite at a man's lungs. Frost lay in the shadows of trees in the plaza, and the peaks of the mountains carried a first white scurf of snow.

Leaving his room at the Exchange Hotel, Frank Darby had said nothing at all to hint that he wouldn't be back within the week. But as he walked briskly along San Francisco Street past the plaza on his way to the stage station, he silently told the town, *Good-bye and good riddance!* He smiled and decided he was pleased, now, at the way things had worked out.

Another man than Darby might have found beauty in this rugged land of red hills studded with piñon. But to him it was the crudest sort of wilderness. Even under clear sunlight, the town itself lacked any grace or charm—a huddle of mud buildings the color of the land itself, with a long and colorful past that meant less than nothing as far as Darby was concerned. He had hated the place from the day he first came here, recommended to Tom Hanlon by business connections in San Francisco.

One thing, and one thing only, could have held him this long—the overpowering attraction of Beth Hanlon, which in time had come to be an obsession. Darby felt for her as he never had about any woman. But he had promised himself that, once they were married, he would take her as far from here as he could get, and they would never see the place again.

Nothing had changed that—only the timing was suddenly a shade different from what he had expected. Instead of waiting for Beth to return to Santa Fe, he would go where she was and tell her of the altered plans. She might be puzzled—even a little startled—but that didn't worry him too much. For experience had given Frank Darby every reason to trust his powers of persuasion.

The Hanlon Stage Line depot stood adjacent to the adobe-walled compound that had served Tom Hanlon for a wagonyard when he was a freighter during the last years of the Santa Fe trade, and later when he had hauled the mails in mule-drawn rigs. Now it housed the big Concords that departed three mornings each week from either end of the line. As Darby walked up, one of the red coaches was just being wheeled from the yard to the front of the depot for loading. The four-horse string was restive, feeling good with the crispness of the morning.

As manager of the Santa Fe office, Frank Darby had no need to buy a ticket; he frequently traveled on company business over this western end of the line. He exchanged pleasantries with the men who were getting the coach ready, saw that his carpetbag was stored in the rear boot, and climbed into the coach. He took the preferred place—on the forward seat with his back to the driver, where dust and rain were least.

For a moment or so, amid a hubbub of preparation going on around the stage, it appeared that he might be the only passenger. But then the door opened again, and someone else swung up onto the iron footplate and then inside. The vehicle swayed gently on its thoroughbraces as the newcomer settled into the opposite seat. And as he looked across the aisle, Darby felt the short hairs at the back of his neck stir in a signal of alarm.

He carefully revealed no sign of this as he nodded to the other man and said, pleasantly enough, "Well—good morning! I didn't know we'd be traveling together."

Ned Archer didn't return the greeting. He would have made a poor poker player. He was, in Darby's opinion, a man entirely without subtlety or imagination—someone who could never hope to disguise whatever emotion he happened to be feeling. Now he stared at Darby across the distance between their seats, and there was hostility in the eyes behind their spectacles, and nervousness in the prim set of his thin-lipped mouth.

Archer was Tom Hanlon's oldest employee—officially his secretary. Actually he was the old man's general factotum and whipping boy, and loyal to the bone—ready to tackle without question any job that might be assigned him, so long as it fell within the range of his limited abilities. He had a narrow face, wiry gray hair, side whiskers, and the perpetual frown of a man trying to understand the world around him.

"And where are you off to?" Darby asked genially, coldly certain he knew the answer before the other gave it.

"Denver."

"Oh? Personal business, I suppose."

"Yes. . . . No!" Archer became confused when he tried to lie, and ended by giving everything away. He scowled and finished lamely: "Something Mr. Hanlon asked me to take care of for him. . . ."

Darby didn't press for more. He didn't need to—Archer couldn't have confirmed his suspicions more directly. Darby carefully smoothed the growing fury from his smile and his voice as he nodded and said, in an offhand manner, "By coincidence I have the same destination. We can keep each other company. We should make connections at Trinidad tomorrow night for the Denver stage."

Archer made no answer, and his frowning stare never changed. Darby let the conversation drop and settled back with a shrug as the coach prepared to roll. The driver and conductor had climbed to their seats, and the horses moved about in anticipation. At the last moment, the coach door opened and two more passengers piled in—an army lieutenant returning to duty at Fort Union, and a portly businessman warmly bundled for the long run to the Hays City railhead in Kansas.

At a shout from the whip, the teams lunged into their harness. Ironshod wheels grated and spun in street gravel as the coach rocked into motion. Frank Darby hardly noticed the boxlike adobe houses of Santa Fe flashing past the stage, the brisk wind whipping dust through the glassless windows, the ancient pueblo dropping away behind them. His thoughts were too bleak and busy with other things.

That bastard Hanlon! he seethed. So the damned old fox hadn't trusted him, after all. He was sending along his flunky to stick close to Darby and make sure he completed his mission and returned to Santa Fe with the promised money. It had been a cruel surprise, and it left Frank Darby with a nasty problem: Something would have to be done about Ned Archer!

Chapter 3

Leaving Hays City, the stage bearing Beth Hanlon followed the new military freight road, laid out earlier that year. It pointed south, straight as a taut string, across the featureless monotony of a flat and endless prairie. Sam Gaines kept his horses moving at an even gait, which made the coach sway easily on its leather thoroughbraces as the miles poured steadily behind them.

The rain had stopped shortly after they left Hays City. Clouds thinned in a widening streak across the center of the sky, and then the sun broke through. The rain-soaked prairie began to steam, forming eerie tendrils that the sun turned into a silver fog, shortening the range of vision to a quarter mile or less.

Sam Gaines squinted ill-humoredly at the eye-punishing glare surrounding them. Gaines, a glum fellow, had taken up the subject of Indian atrocities. One story led to another—a detailed recital of every incident he had ever heard of wagon trains being attacked, army details waylaid and massacred, settlers and way-station operators besieged and murdered, stock driven off, and buildings put to the torch along the road to Santa Fe. Seated beside him on the high front boot, Clay Reiner let him talk—he had heard these reports, had checked them out, and then had formed his own opinion as to which were authentic and which were the garbled invention of frontier storytelling.

Uneasy at the blinding smear of sunlight in the fog through which the stage was traveling, Gaines remarked sourly, "Just now would be a dandy time for them devils to come busting out of this stuff. They could be right on top of us before we even seen them!"

"They wouldn't be able to see us much better," Reiner pointed out. "And anyway, I haven't heard reports of any war parties in this area lately." He added dryly, "Besides, maybe you forgot—we have us a new treaty with the Plains tribes, drawn up and signed just last month over at Medicine Lodge. It's supposed to take care of all that."

He anticipated the angry snort from the grizzled driver beside him. "Sure—but for how long? About as long as all them other treaties!"

"It should mean a breathing space, at least. Maybe enough to get *this* stage through without trouble."

"And without no calv'ry escort, neither!" the driver retorted, with an angry shake of his head. "What the hell's the military supposed to be doing out here, *I* want to know, if it ain't to keep the trails open and traffic moving safe? Instead, now they've gone and pulled all their escorts off and are sending us out *nekkid*! Maybe the army's happy as hell with their treaty. Personally, I don't admire being the settin' duck to prove they was wrong!"

"In any event," Reiner said, "there's nothing much you or I can do about it. And I'll appreciate it if you don't say any of this where the passengers might hear you and get upset. Myself, I'd rather not waste worrying until I know for sure I have something to worry about."

Gaines cast him a sidelong look. "You ain't even a little bit uneasy? I'd think you would be, knowing you got the old man's whole family aboard!"

Reiner frowned. He wasn't ready to admit, even to himself, just how concerned he was. He was particularly aware, too, of the presence of Beth Hanlon in the stagecoach below them. But all he said, a little gruffly, was, "Only a fool would ever take this job for granted. We've got to be ready for anything to happen, anytime we take a coach out. But there's no point stewing over it."

The other man swore at one of his wheelers—the pair of horses nearest the stage. After a moment, he suggested dryly, "Seems to me, in your place I'd be stewing some over that sonofabitch McRae! He don't mean for anyone in this outfit to forget, even for a minute, about him being Tom Hanlon's brother-in-law! He figures it gives him special privileges—and maybe it does. I'm just glad I ain't the one that's stuck with him! You reckon you can get clear to Santa Fe without having to straighten him out somewhere along the line?"

"If the time comes when I have to, then I suppose I will."

"You do, and he's the kind who'll never let you hear the end of it! You can bet he'll go straight to the old man himself. He'll have your job if he can."

"His privilege to try. . . ."

Another hour passed and the fog gradually lifted, burned away by the sun. A colorless world turned bright and tawny beneath a wide and deep-blue ceiling of sky. Reiner stripped off his poncho and stowed it in the spacious boot beneath the seat, then took the reins for a moment so the driver could do likewise. A sharp November wind whipped at them, chasing cloud shadows across the prairie as the coach crawled along the twin ribbons of the military road, lost in an immensity of land.

Presently a cluster of sod buildings and corrals began to take shape ahead of them, and as they neared the station, Sam Gaines fished up a battered brass horn and blasted a few thin notes to alert the stationmen to the coming of the stage. At once there was activity among the buildings, and as the stage drew nearer, two span of horses were run out of the corrals, put into harness, and brought up to take the place of the animals on the pole.

As Gaines stood on the brake, the stage came tooling in and skidded to a stop, wheels and hooves raising sheets of muddy slop from puddles of rainwater around the work area. Stockmen were already on hand for the smooth operation of unhooking and replacing the teams, working under the eagle eye of the driver. While all this was going on, Clay Reiner stepped down to check on his passengers.

The coach door opened, and Harris McRae came crawling stiffly out. He gave Reiner a challenging look. "Only stretching my legs," he said curtly. "Any objections? It's tiresome just sitting there."

"You'd better plan to get used to it," Reiner told him. "And don't go wandering off. We've still got lost time to make up. We'll only be here long enough to change teams—about five minutes. Soon as it's done, we roll."

McRae gave him an angry stare. He looked at the work the station hands were doing and saw the job was already near completion. With an angry shrug, he turned and clambered back inside the vehicle, dropping heavily onto the leather-padded seat next to his sister, Mary Hanlon.

"Everyone in there all right?" Clay Reiner asked.

He got assurances from the women. When he looked at Beth, she regarded him with what he took to be a troubled frown, but this quickly cleared and she smiled as she said, "We're fine, Clay."

Young Johnny Winfield was leaning from one of the rear windows, craning ahead as he tried to get a better view of the changing of the teams. It struck Reiner as being the first time he had seen him show any real interest or seen any break in the unnatural apathy that bothered him about the youngster. He was prompted to suggest, "Now that it's stopped raining, Johnny, would you like to come up on the box with Sam and me? You can see a lot better from there, and you might find it interesting how Sam works with his horses."

The boy looked first to his mother and got Amelia Winfield's consenting nod. To Reiner he then said, "All right," but without much show of enthusiasm.

Reiner didn't give him time to reconsider. He opened the door and hustled the boy outside, saying, "Let's go, then." He gave him a hand up to the box. Afterward,

34

having exchanged a few words with the men of the station, he swung up himself. The fresh horses were moving about restlessly in the harness as the old teams were led away, and Sam Gaines already was sorting out the leather reins. Having relinquished his own place to Johnny, Reiner took a seat on the edge of the coach roof behind them. Sam waved a farewell salute to the stationmen and then, with a whoop and a holler, got his new teams into motion.

In minutes, the huddle of sod buildings—with its men who led a lonely existence that was broken only by the brief arrivals and departures of the big, red Concords—was swallowed up in the immensity of the prairie. Once more, the stage riders felt only the press of the wind, the monotonous rhythm of hooves and wheels, and the ruts of the road stretching ahead of them.

Reiner filled his pipe and got it going, then settled back to enjoy a smoke. Plainly, Johnny was fascinated by the expert way Sam Gaines handled the coach, with the reins threaded through the leather-toughened fingers of one hand. Reiner knew that Sam, for all his gruffness of manner, was secretly pleased to be able to show off by answering the questions the youngster threw at him. He thought Johnny seemed disappointed when he got a negative reply on asking, "Are you going to be driving, Sam, all the way to New Mexico?"

"Oh, heck no! You'll be changing drivers every forty miles or so. Mr. Reiner's the only one who'll be staying with you the whole distance." Giving a nod to the leather whip coiled on the seat beside him, he suggested, "You reckon you're any good with that thing? Let's see if you can give the near wheeler a little dust-up, to put him in the collar. . . ."

Johnny probably had been itching to lay hands on the coils of supple, braided rawhide. He could hardly know that he'd just been accorded a rare honor—only Clay was aware just how jealously Sam guarded that whip from anyone's hands but his own. The boy was clumsy in his first attempts, and Sam gave him some pointers. Then Johnny began to get some of the hang of it—enough, at least, so that after several tries he actually managed to snap the popper close enough to the offending wheeler to make the animal waggle its ears and quicken its pace.

Sam rewarded him with a shout. "Damn good, boy! That pesky Ol' Blue just likes to get out of his share of the pulling. . . ." And the youngster seemed to swell with his approval.

"John Winfield," Reiner said suddenly. "Would that be your father's name, too?" The boy turned quickly, shooting him an unreadable look. His manner seemed to close down before he answered with a short nod.

"I just wondered," Reiner went on. "I was at Shiloh—got wounded there. But I remember that a Lieutenant John Winfield in a Pennsylvania outfit got himself decorated and promoted for heroism in action during that fight. I heard the name again later—many times. Seems like he was a colonel when the war ended. If that was your pa, you must be mighty proud." But this time he got neither a look nor a nod in answer. After a moment, he went on: "Could be a different man, of course. I never heard mention of him being stationed at Fort Union."

Johnny was looking straight ahead at the ruts of the stage road sweeping toward them from beyond the heads of the lead team. The set of his shoulders was stiffly unyielding.

"He ain't been there very long," the boy muttered finally. "Anyway, Pa ain't a colonel now. That was only what the army calls a brevet rating. Now that the war's over, he's back to lieutenant again."

"Well," Reiner said, "I surely intend to look him up. I'd enjoy meeting an honest-to-God hero. . . ."

There was no reply from Johnny, and reluctantly Clay let the matter drop.

* * *

The noon halt was at a home station, its buildings more substantial than at the others they had seen. Here, meals were served, and there even were accommodations of a sort for travelers who might want to lay over and wait for a later coach. It was a little past noon when they brought the place in sight and came barreling in, the squawk of Sam's horn once more warning of their arrival.

The rough forage of stage-line victuals—likely as not canned tomatoes, beans, biscuits, strong black coffee, dried apple pie, and perhaps a platter of venison steaks—already would be dished up and waiting. Clay swung open the coach door, waited while the passengers alighted and headed for the station, and noted wryly that Harris McRae appeared to have taken charge of the attractive Amelia Winfield. He helped her down the iron step and hovered over her, taking her elbow and chatting in the most familiar manner as he herded her across the muddy work area. At any rate, it gave the man something to interest him besides his dislike of Clay Reiner!

Next to him, Beth Hanlon asked, "Clay, may I speak to you a moment?"

He turned quickly. "Why, certainly." Her expression, beneath the edge of the fur cap, made him add, "Is something the matter?"

"It's my uncle." Her manner was serious. "I've been wanting to apologize—because I know *he* never will!"

Reiner stared. "You've got nothing to apologize for."

"Please," she insisted. "I want to say this. . . . I'm really ashamed of him! I can't help it that he's part of my family, or that he probably doesn't even realize the effect he has on people. The thing is, it wouldn't matter to him if he did! He just doesn't care about people's feelings. Did you notice how he's playing up to that nice Mrs. Winfield? No difference to *him* that she's got a husband waiting, or that she'd surely much rather he left her alone. To him, nothing in the world counts except Harris McRae!"

Clay had already marked the man down as a pompous

boor, but he felt constrained to point out, "You have to admit, he's concerned at least for you and your mother. He's making quite a sacrifice to come on this trip, and all because he feels you need him."

"I tell myself that," Beth said with a sigh, "but I can't help wondering if it isn't as much for his own benefit as for anybody else. If Pa should happen to—" she faltered over the words "—to not get well, Uncle Harris would certainly want to be right there, not just to look after the family's interests but to see if maybe he could do himself some good! Oh, I'm not being fair, I suppose," she went on, with a despairing gesture. "But just about everything that man says or does simply gets my goat! Including the way he treats *you*, Clay!"

"Don't let that bother you. *I* don't."

"But it isn't right," she insisted. "Uncle Harris has been lucky with that store of his in Kansas City, and somehow it makes him think he can look down his nose at anyone who works on another man's payroll. Well, you and I know—and so does Pa—just how big a role you've had in keeping this stage line going. The way Uncle Harris talks to you not only makes me ashamed, it makes me mad! Especially when he tries to threaten you with losing your job!"

Her eyes flashed, and her jaw had an angry set to it. Touched by the sincerity in her voice, which almost trembled with emotion, Clay was moved to rest a hand on her shoulder. "Believe me," he said, "Harris McRae's threats are about the least of all the things that scare me. So please, don't worry about this." He added with sincerity, "Though I do appreciate you wanting to say it."

Now that she had spoken, Beth seemed to have satisfied the angry urges that moved her. She suddenly acted a little self-conscious about her own behavior. She gave Clay a swift look and a tremulous smile. "I guess I—just had to get it off my chest. I hope you understand." And with that she was gone.

Watching her walk toward the station, Reiner was engulfed in a flood of emotions. He had known Beth Hanlon all through his years working for her father. He had seen her grow from leggy adolescence into a sunny-hearted and maturely beautiful young woman. He couldn't even remember when it was he fell in love with her, except that it had been long before Frank Darby appeared on the scene.

It had been no easy thing to see an attraction form and develop between Beth and the man who became his rival. It would be too much to say that news of their engagement had destroyed Clay's hopes, because actually he had never held any. There was nothing put on about Beth—nothing but the most sincere regard for an old friend like Clay Reiner. Still, as a mere employee of her father, he had never let himself imagine he stood any real chance with her, or that he deserved one.

Frank Darby, on the other hand, possessed every quality Clay felt he lacked himself: sharp intelligence, good looks and education, and a culture and polish that suited Tom Hanlon's handsome daughter. Seeing them together made Reiner feel very rough edged and un-mannered—a man trained on dusty trails who made a poor showing in contrast to his rival. As far as he could see, there clearly was no contest, and he deliberately had put a rein on his own feelings. No one was ever going to say he was a poor sport.

But still it touched Clay deeply to think that Beth would go out of her way to apologize and try to make amends for her uncle's behavior. He knew it was a moment he would never forget. . . .

Chapter 4

Two years earlier, in 1865, Fort Dodge had been established to keep a check on the Plains tribes—Comanche, Kiowa, and Arapaho—in the vicinity of the lower Arkansas River. The first troops had lived in roofed-over holes dug into the river's north bank. Now there was a parade ground rimmed by a hospital, barracks, headquarters, and other structures built of sod and of limestone from a quarry several miles to the north. But for all that, it was still a place where soldiers and civilians led a bleak, lonely, and dangerous existence.

Prior to the construction of the fort, a Hanlon Stage Line way station near the site had been burned to the ground by Indians. It had been rebuilt and now stood within the protective shadow of the military installation. The lights of the fort and station played across the flats as the westbound coach came rolling in, pulling up sharply. The night air held a real chill, and ground frost sparkled in the glow of the coach lamps and the lantern that hung from a pole in the station compound. As the familiar routine of changing teams proceeded, Clay Reiner swung down a little stiffly from his place on the forward boot, where he had managed to get an hour or so of fitful sleep.

There was no sound from within the stage, though Reiner thought he saw someone finger aside a window shield for a brief look into the station yard. The long day of travel had taken its toll on the people inside. Bundled up in blankets and fur robes supplied by the stage line, and with

41

leather window curtains rolled down against the night chill, they were either asleep or too numbed with fatigue to stir.

It was in moments like this—especially with Beth Hanlon so near and so wholly vulnerable—that Reiner felt most keenly his responsibility for all those people in the coach. They had placed their lives in his hands, trusting him to get them safely through the days and miles that lay ahead. This was a sobering thought—and yet it was one that inspired him with the importance of the job he had undertaken. . . .

The teams soon were changed, with the usual smooth efficiency that the Hanlon Stage Line trained into its crews. Reiner had barely settled again in his place when the current driver—a couple of stations back, Sam Gaines, with his whip and his battered bugle, had been relieved—yelled his horses into their collars, and the coach swayed again into motion. They passed the lights of Fort Dodge and were on their way, following the north bank of the Arkansas.

Sometime later, a wink of light showed ahead. It grew as it neared, gradually splitting to become the lamps of another stage coming toward them. This would be the eastbound coach that had left Santa Fe on Monday morning. After what seemed an interminable stretch of time, the other vehicle, with its ambling horses and pale blobs of faces on the forward boot, loomed up out of the darkness. With calls of greeting from the drivers, both outfits halted under the immensity of the starlit sky. Window shields were pulled aside as the passengers from Hays City and Santa Fe peered curiously at one another.

The messenger on the eastbound coach was a man named Walsh. Recognizing Tom Hanlon's troubleshooter, he exclaimed, "Hey, Reiner! I didn't know you were bringing one through."

While the teams stomped and jingled their harnesses, there was the usual exchange of news about the section of

road each party had recently traveled. All was quiet along
the upper Arkansas, Walsh reported—no trouble of any
kind, despite the withdrawal of military escorts in the
wake of the Medicine Grove treaty. He added, "You got
one little problem waiting for you, though. At Mule Creek
Station."

"Oh? What's wrong there?"

"What you might have expected. That damned Swede."

"Bregman?" Reiner asked sharply, and the driver beside him swore under his breath. "What's he done?"

"Last evening when we come through," Walsh said,
"he was fighting the bottle, and clear out of hand."

"Where would he get liquor? Tom Hanlon doesn't
allow it at his stations."

"Well, he got it somewhere. Apparently some wagon
freighter left him off a jug. Anyway, Lute Geraghty says
he knows nothing about it. Geraghty was scared to death.
Bregman's supposed to be working for him, but it's plain
to see he can't noway manage the fellow when he's got
blood in his eye."

The driver of Reiner's coach, Bud Street, was one of
the newer men with the company, but thoroughly experi-
enced. He said sourly, "I knew it was a bad mistake of
Hanlon's, hiring that Nels Bregman. Sober, nobody can
deny he's a good hand with horses. But he can't manage
the stuff that comes in jugs! I ran across a fellow who saw
him in action once in Denver. According to him, Bregman
and some other drunk got in a fight over nothing, and the
big Swede come near breaking the other man's neck with
his bare hands before the crowd was able to pull the two
of them apart!"

Clay Reiner reserved comment. He asked Walsh,
"Just what did you see at Mule Creek? What happened?"

"Why, the big man was walking around as though he
owned the place—jug in hand and a six-shooter stuck
behind his belt. When Lute Geraghty told him to give a
hand changing teams, Bregman cussed him out to a point

where I almost thought he was getting ready to use that gun on him. I think Geraghty thought so, too. He backed down fast. The way the thing ended up, I had to pitch in myself and help wrangle fresh teams out of the corral and into the harness. Hell, one of them almost kicked my head in!"

"And what was Bregman up to during this time?"

"Prowling around—jeering at us and threatening the passengers. I could see Geraghty was scared white and shaking so bad he could hardly work the harness. He told me Bregman had started in drinking that morning, and it had been getting worse ever since. Honest to God, I hated to go off and leave the two of them. I told Geraghty he should arm himself, and if he had to in order to protect himself, he should shoot and not hesitate about shooting to kill!"

Walsh's driver spoke up. "There was nothing we could do, Reiner. We had to keep rolling. For all we know, one or the other of 'em may be dead by this time. If they ain't, looks like you got a job on your hands. *Something* has to be done about the sonofabitch. He's dangerous!"

"We'll see," Reiner said shortly, and after a last brief exchange, gave Bud Street a sign to continue. With shouts and the popping of whips, both drivers got their teams in motion. The coaches lurched ahead and drew swiftly apart, and the night swept them up into its chill silence.

Street snapped the leathers at his teams. He told Reiner darkly, "You listen to me and you'll get rid of that Swede, fast! Before he kills somebody. And hire a new stationmaster while you're at it. Lute Geraghty is too damned lightweight and easygoing for anybody's good, if he can't keep his own stockman in line."

"We'll see," Reiner repeated, his tone noncommittal.

The driver swore. "You realize, what Walsh was telling us about happened hours ago. It's gonna be midmorning before we reach Mule Creek Station. God only knows what we may find by then!"

Clay Reiner had to admit he was right.

*   *   *

Dawn came bleakly—a thin line of light across the flat horizon, and then the stars paling as the sky turned a burnished steel. In the grainy light, Beth Hanlon looked around at her fellow passengers. She knew the other people had rested as fitfully as she, trying somehow to sleep bolt upright on thinly padded seats. She also knew, from experience, that by the end of a second day of unbroken travel they would be ready enough to sleep, even under these circumstances.

It was age that made the difference. Young Johnny Winfield had slept more soundly than anyone else, while Mary Hanlon awoke looking gray of face. And her brother grimaced and made complaining grunts as he straightened his cramped limbs and shifted position. When Beth gave her companions a cheerful "Good morning," her uncle Harris merely gave her a scowl and a shrug.

Beth turned to peer past the leather window cover at the autumn-brown prairie grass combed and flattened by the wind, and at the flat surface of the river under rising streamers of mist. Overhead, the sky was a clear, wintry blue that paled at the horizon. She listened to the desultory talk of the others, her own thoughts abstracted and busy with matters that concerned her.

When they pulled into another of the lonely stations—each seeming more bleak and isolated than the one before—Clay Reiner opened the door of the coach to say cheerily, "I hope everybody survived! Nights like these can seem pretty long, until you get used to them." All but Johnny, who still slept in his corner of the rear seat, and the sullen Harris McRae returned the greeting. And they seemed pleased enough to accept an invitation to step outside and stretch their cramped limbs while the teams were being changed.

Beth found an opportunity to draw Reiner aside for a moment and ask the question that had been troubling her. "Last night, when we met that other coach, I wasn't able to hear everything that was said, but I got an impression there might be some sort of trouble. . . ."

"Nothing for you to worry about," he reassured her. "A little dispute between the fellows at Mule Creek Station up ahead, that's all. It's something I'll have to try and settle, once we get there."

Beth studied his face, not wholly convinced. "You're really sure that's all it is?"

"I don't think it will amount to anything. It's part of my job to see it doesn't." But he hesitated then, and she was sure that a deeper concern surfaced as he added more slowly, as though reluctant to say the words, "Of course, if anything *should* go wrong—now or at any time during this journey—well, I'm hoping you'll look after your mother. And don't take any unnecessary chances yourself. Far as I'm concerned, the most important thing is that nothing should happen to *you*. To either of you," he added quickly.

"Why, thank you, Clay!" she said earnestly. That was real loyalty, she thought—loyalty to the company, to Tom Hanlon, and to Tom's womenfolk. And yet, something she saw in his face left her staring after him in growing puzzlement as he turned to walk away. Somehow, she wasn't quite sure he had said all he wanted to.

Despite his assurances to Beth, Clay Reiner was taking very seriously the news from Walsh. He knew it wasn't likely the man had exaggerated. These lonely stations, strung out along the stage road that threaded through the emptiness of the plains, were poised perilously on a thin edge of danger, and any sort of mishap could quickly turn to disaster. This was especially true of the swing stations like Mule Creek, often held down by no more than a couple of men whose job it was to supply fresh teams to the coaches and who had almost no other human contact from one month to the next. In such isolation, monotony and danger became almost unbearable, and tempers could fray.

Reiner found himself peering anxiously ahead, his eyes slitted against the steady wind that swept these flat and empty plains. The way station showed first as a dark blot against the dry grass of the Arkansas River bottoms. It grew and became a huddle of low-roofed soddies beside a cottonwood pole corral with a few head of stock running inside. Otherwise, there was no sign of movement—not even when Bud Street brought his coach to a rocking halt in the wheel-scored compound between main building and tack barn. In the stillness, Reiner looked around with growing concern, hearing only the ceaseless breath of the wind—and then, from the barn, a sudden crash as though something had been overturned.

He jumped down to the ground, pausing to warn the passengers they should stay where they were. He walked over the hard ruts to the barn, and as he did he found that his fingers, as though of their own volition, had sought and rested on the butt of his holstered gun.

More noises greeted him. It sounded almost as if the barn was being ransacked. He saw that a harness rack had been upended and lay half across the doorway, in a tangle of equipment that made Reiner's mouth harden at the sight of it. He heard someone call his name then, and turned around as Lute Geraghty came hurrying toward him, bareheaded and coatless, from the direction of the station building.

Geraghty wasn't a big man. He was a fellow in his mid-forties, with a ready grin and a shock of rusty hair that wouldn't stay in place. His usual expression suggested an equable temper and an easygoing nature that seemed suited to the lonely job of a stationmaster.

Just now his good nature appeared to have slipped somewhat. He looked harried and distraught, and without preliminaries Clay Reiner said, "I met the eastbound stage, which came through here yesterday. Walsh said you had some trouble you didn't seem able to handle." He jerked

47

his head toward the racket inside the barn. "Sounds to me it could still be going on."

"Yeah." Geraghty ran a hand distractedly through his unruly mop of hair. "I suppose you heard what it's all about. Nels Bregman! He got hold of a jug somewhere—I didn't even know until it was too late."

"You should have taken it away from him."

"I should have at least tried," the other man agreed. "I realize that now. But I thought, what the hell, he'd take a couple of snorts and settle for that. I didn't know he was one of those birds who once they get started, there's no way they can quit till they've put away everything in sight!" There was another loud crash from within the barn. Then Lute continued, "And as he got drunk, he got mean! I'd never seen any hint of that all the months I've had him here working for me. It didn't take long, though, for me to know that he wasn't gonna be *talked* out of that jug! I'd have had to use a gun."

Reiner snapped, "Then why didn't you?"

"It woulda meant shooting him, Clay!" Geraghty shook his head unhappily. "Nothing else would have done the job. And—hell! I can't see killing a man just because he has a thirst! What I did," he went on, "was I just stayed out of the way and gave him a chance to run down. Finally he did, and fell over asleep. I was able to get the jug then, and I emptied it out, figuring when he came to he'd suppose he drunk it all. I only left a couple of swallows—hair of the dog, to help ease the hangover I knew he'd wake up with this morning. And just to be sure, I went out here to the barn and poked around. And sure enough, I found he had *another* jug hid—a reserve. So I took it. Trouble is, this morning he had that last drink and it only set him off again! I couldn't get food, coffee, nothing into him. He headed right for the barn, and ever since he's been looking for that second jug. This one." And he held up the demijohn he had been carrying in one hand. "I was just about ready to go ahead and give it to him, before he wrecks the place trying to find where he hid it. Maybe with a little more of this down him, he'll simply pass out. Otherwise," he admitted heavily, "I honest to God don't know *what* to do!"

"That's just your trouble, Geraghty," Reiner told him sharply. "You always look for the easiest way to solve any problem. In this case you couldn't have chosen worse! Well, come along," he added. "This thing has already gone too far. It has to be settled—now!"

Reiner was keenly aware of the people in the coach, who were watching in silence as he and Geraghty approached the tack barn. He heard a heavy packing case or something go over inside the barn, and the Swede's hoarse breathing. When Reiner called Bregman's name, the sounds broke off. Then, with a shuffling of boots, a man came out of the shadows and halted just within the doorway, scowling.

The Swede was a big one. His bullet-shaped head, with its unshorn yellow hair and pale brows and whiskers, loomed above Reiner. He had a torso and limbs to match. Apparently unmindful of the chill, he was in his shirt sleeves with the cuffs rolled back, revealing thick forearms furred with hairs so blond as to look nearly white. Blue eyes, bloodshot now, squinted into the brighter sunlight beyond the open door.

"Well, Bregman," Reiner said, pitching his voice to cut through the fog of cheap snake-juice whiskey. "You've made a real mess here, haven't you? Is this what you're looking for?" And he indicated the jug carried by Lute Geraghty.

Nels Bregman looked at the jug; it seemed to take a moment for him to identify it. When he did, his head jerked up and he cried out thickly, "By gar—yes! You give me that!"

"No chance!" Reiner snapped. "You know Tom Hanlon's rule against any kind of liquor at his stations—even if you don't follow it!" He looked at the station agent. "Geraghty, take the thing away somewhere and smash it!"

Geraghty stared at him for just a moment, and then

quickly nodded and turned to follow the order. Seeing that, Bregman shouted, "Is mine!" and lunged forward. But Reiner was waiting, and he stopped the Swede with a hand against his chest. It was like trying to shove a wall, but Bregman was a shade uncertain on his boots, and he was halted and driven back a step.

But that triggered a sudden roar of rage from the man, directed at Reiner himself. And then Nels Bregman started for him, one huge fist rising.

Chapter 5

Knowing the big Swede's fist could hurt, but also knowing he was in for a fight whether he wanted one or not, Clay Reiner checked an impulse to backwater. He stood his ground as Nels Bregman came at him, only taking a quick side-stepping motion that he hoped would cause the clumsy blow to miss. He lifted his left arm in time to deflect the main force of it, though the impact made his arm go numb to the elbow. Then he countered with a swing of his own fist, striking the big man in the face and halting him where he stood.

Bregman's face had flushed to a brick red. Lute Geraghty and the confiscated whiskey jug seemed to have been forgotten in his fury at the man in front of him. Reiner, watching those bloodshot eyes for hints of the next move, was aware of voices yelling encouragement—Bud Street and young Johnny Winfield shouting excitedly. Yonder, Geraghty hovered in an agony of indecision as he tried to think of a way to help.

Reiner didn't want any help. This was *his* problem to deal with now. Trying to penetrate the fog of whiskey and rage, he told the big man sharply, "Cut it out, Bregman! You're only making matters worse!" The Swede probably never heard him. Suddenly one of those big hands reached out and, before Reiner could move away, closed on his shoulder—the one still partially crippled from a sniper's bullet. The pain drew a gasp from him, and knowledge of the damage those meaty fingers could cause made Reiner pivot violently in an effort to wrench free.

He succeeded, but one bootheel caught in the hard wheel ruts underfoot, and he lost his balance and went down, managing to catch himself on one knee to keep from falling prone. When he glanced up, his vision was filled by the shape of the big man closing in on him. The thought of those heavy cowhide boots stomping him into the ground kept Reiner moving, and somehow he managed to scramble out of the way and roll back and up onto his feet.

Bregman, having overshot his mark, turned with him and swung again. A glancing blow struck the side of Reiner's head and made it ring like a bell. He shook his head and, seeing an opening, leaped into it. He hit the Swede and saw blood smear one broad cheek. Then, with a fierce shove, Reiner's shoulder butted the man in the center of his thick chest and drove him backward. The edge of the barn doorway at his back stopped him. Next moment, stung by the painful blow that nearly blinded him, Bregman went for his gun.

If Reiner hadn't seen the danger, a piercing cry from Beth Hanlon as she watched from the coach window would have alerted him. He didn't hesitate, but didn't reach for his own revolver. Driven by the thought of peril to the people in the coach in the event of wild and undirected gunfire, Clay rushed in, groping for the hand that held Bregman's six-shooter. It was like grappling with a fence post. With all his strength, Reiner shoved the arm aside, and Bregman's knuckles slammed the doorjamb with such force that his revolver popped out of his fingers. Then Reiner threw a blow, with all his weight behind it, at the side of Bregman's bullet-shaped head.

It was a lucky punch—a hard one that caught Bregman squarely on the hinge of the jaw. His head was flung to the side, the yellow hair tossing wildly. Reiner stepped back as the big man fell heavily to his knees and then, with a sound like a heavy sigh, sprawled across the doorway and lay unmoving. Scarcely believing, Clay Reiner stood panting as he unconsciously rubbed his aching shoulder.

There was a hubbub of excited voices at the stage, and now Bud Street and Lute Geraghty rushed over to Reiner—Geraghty still lugging the confiscated whiskey jug. The driver picked up the revolver that had fallen from Bregman's fingers. "You all right, boss?" he demanded.

Reiner, kneading his shoulder, nodded briefly. The man he had felled was already stirring feebly, and Geraghty said, "So's Nels. He should be coming around in a few minutes." Geraghty appeared badly shaken. Looking at him thoughtfully, Reiner reached a decision.

He chose his words carefully, his manner stern as he announced, "Lute, it looks like I'm going to have to count on you to keep Bregman in line, and at least try to get *some* work out of him, until I've had a chance to send you out a replacement."

The station agent gave him a look. He hesitated. "You're firing him?"

Bud Street gave a snort. "Jeez!" he cried. "After *this*? How the hell could you ask?"

"Maybe one of the other stations can spare us a man for the time being," Reiner went on crisply. "One way or another, I want to be rid of Bregman as fast as we can get him off the place!"

The agent was gnawing at his lip. "Mr. Reiner . . ." he began, then managed to blurt out, "there—isn't there any way . . . I mean, you couldn't maybe give him another chance?"

"You ain't serious!" Street exclaimed.

Ignoring him, the stationmaster plowed ahead. "To tell you the truth, Mr. Reiner, it would be like another chance for both of us. This has been my fault as much as Bregman's. Hell, it was my job to keep such things from happening—like him sneaking that whiskey onto the station. I was supposed to be in *charge*! I guess I just didn't pay close enough attention."

"It would look that way," Reiner agreed curtly.

Geraghty drew a breath, then continued earnestly. "Nels always struck me as a decent sort, and he's been a hard worker. I think he can be again, once he sobers up. If I was to make you a promise—if I guarantee Nels Bregman will never get his hands on another jug of rotgut as long as the two of us are at Mule Creek Station—would you maybe change your mind and let him stay on?"

Reiner appeared to debate his answer before he said pointedly, "Are you sure you want to· shoulder the responsibility?"

The man nodded. "Don't you think it's about time? This *is* my responsibility—and if I'd only worked at it better, the trouble never would have come up. I figure I owe it to Nels to try and keep him from losing his job over it—and to the stage line, to keep it from losing a good stock handler!"

"Well, all right then," Reiner muttered, trying to make his decision sound reluctant. "We'll see how it works out. Meanwhile, Bud'll get rid of that jug. And you keep Bregman's gun," he added sternly. "Let him know you'll use it on him if he forces you to! Don't run any more risks."

"Oh, I won't! I've learned my lesson. . . ."

While Geraghty and a dubious Bud Street silently exchanged the jug and the weapon, Reiner kneeled down to see how Nels Bregman was. The big man was coming around. At Reiner's touch he groaned and managed to roll over, and Reiner took him by the shoulders and helped him to a sitting position against the adobe wall of the tack barn. All the fight had been knocked out of the Swede. He lifted a hand, touched his fingers to the cut that had been opened on his cheek, and stared dumbly at the blood he found on them.

Satisfied, Reiner got to his feet and looked again at

Lute Geraghty. "He isn't hurt bad. One of the first jobs I want him to do is to clean up the mess he's made of the barn. And *he's* to do it, you understand? Don't help him."

The stationmaster nodded. With that, Reiner returned to the stage where the passengers had been observing all this in silence. Beth and Johnny Winfield had gotten out of the coach. The boy looked wild-eyed with excitement, while Beth, her face drained colorless at what she had been witnessing, rested a hand on Johnny's shoulder as though to hold him back. In the coach windows, Reiner saw Amelia Winfield and Beth's mother and her uncle Harris. It was the latter's scowl that made him say, in apology, "I'm damned sorry this had to happen. Sorrier still that you folks had to see me use my fists on him. We'll be on our way as soon as Lute and I can get these teams changed. . . ."

And he turned away from the shocked and disapproving looks he knew must be on their faces.

There was no disapproval, at least, in young Johnny Winfield. The teams had been switched and the coach had rolled away again, leaving behind the pair of men who must somehow mend their relationship and put the station back in functioning order. But even now the boy was unable to contain his open admiration for what Clay Reiner had done. "Golly!" he cried to everyone inside the coach. "Did you see how he went after that big guy with nothing but his bare hands? He took the gun off him—and just laid him out cold!"

Harris McRae answered in a tone that dripped with scorn. "Oh, yes. We saw, all right! I swear, I don't know what the fellow had in mind, unless it was to impress us with how brave and tough he is!" He looked askance at his sister. "Mary, that husband of yours always was a rough-neck. It's obvious this man Reiner is exactly the sort of heavy-handed brute he'd want running his stage line for him!"

His comments were too much for Beth. Suddenly, she no longer could bear in silence her irritation with her uncle. Her head jerked up and her eyes flashed with indignation as she cried, "Uncle Harris! I can't sit here and listen to you say that—it isn't true! If you call Clay Reiner a brute, it's because you don't begin to understand what went on back there! He did exactly what he had to. He used his fists because that was the only thing a man like Nels Bregman could be counted on to respect. And then, by threatening to fire him, he forced that other man—Geraghty—to admit to himself he hadn't done *his* job right, and promise from then on he'd make Bregman toe the mark. If you'd only had your eyes open, instead of blinded by prejudice toward Clay, you'd have seen that's exactly what he was aiming for. He saved the stage line two good workers—and on this frontier, there aren't many to spare!"

She was breathing hard when she finished, suddenly abashed at her own words. McRae had drawn up stiffly as he heard her out, his mouth gone tight at the corners. But if he was stung by what she had said, he gave no sign of having changed his opinion. Only one thing seemed to have registered with him, and his manner was coldly disapproving as he retorted, "So it's *Clay*, is it? Interesting!" He turned to his sister. "Mary, I thought you told me this girl was engaged to another young fellow, in Santa Fe. A college chap, you said—a man with a good head for business and a promising future. Could there be something going on here that you don't know about?"

Beth gasped as she felt her face grow warm. She tried to stammer a protest, but the words wouldn't come. She could only whip her head around, lips tight, and stare in angry confusion at the prairie rolling past her window.

Frank Darby's nerves were stretched thin. It was early evening of his second day of unrelenting travel, cooped up in a stagecoach with the unimaginative Ned

Archer and two other passengers. He had long since given up attempting conversation. Archer said little, but his silences were eloquent enough. Darby would catch the man staring at him with a glittering intensity, only to let his glance slide away when their eyes happened to meet. Darby knew the fellow was studying him, and it removed any doubt as to just what Archer knew, or why Tom Hanlon had put him aboard this stage.

Though he had only contempt for a toady like Archer, Darby knew perfectly well the man could spell disaster. Archer had his orders, and they were certain to involve sticking to Frank Darby like a leech until the supposed business in Denver was completed and he returned to Santa Fe with the promised money. The question was, what was to be done about him?

By now they had crossed Raton Pass into Colorado Territory, had taken a meal stop at the tollgate house maintained by the famed Uncle Dick Wootton, and were still bearing north through early dusk, heading for lower country along the Purgatoire River. At Trinidad the stage road would turn northeast toward Timpas Creek, eventually to pick up the Arkansas River and head on in the direction of Kansas City. And at Trinidad, Archer would be expecting them both to leave this coach and transfer to another stage line, Denver bound. It meant that Darby must soon face a decision that could no longer be put off.

He was working up his plan when a sudden jarring crash sent the passengers grabbing for tug straps, crying out as they fought to keep from being hurled from their seats. The coach rocked violently on its thoroughbraces as it halted, and they could hear the driver and messenger swearing as they scrambled down from the boot.

Darby pushed aside the leather window cover and leaned out, demanding to know what had happened. He got no answer at first. The problem, whatever it might be, was being examined with the aid of a couple of hastily lighted lanterns. The passengers waited in the settling chill, and a night wind whistled eerily through the rocks that crowded the stage road. Presently the messenger came tramping back, lantern in hand, and gave the news.

"Our wheel hit a boulder in the road," he announced roughly. "Looks like we cracked a couple of spokes and maybe bent the axle. We're an hour out of Trinidad—gives us no choice but to cripple on in as best we can, and try not to break down before we get there."

A man who had boarded the stage back at Las Vegas exclaimed, "Hell, we'll never make any time!"

"Let's just hope we make the next station!"

The driver climbed to his seat, straightened his teams out, and started the coach inching gingerly forward, testing the damaged wheel. Ned Archer seemed the only one not too greatly concerned about the mishap. "No great matter to me what time we get in," he said smugly. "The Denver stage doesn't leave till morning."

Even so, it was an uncomfortable trip, crawling those last miles with the thermometer dropping steadily. When the coach finally pulled up in front of the Colorado Hotel just before eight o'clock and the passengers debarked, they saw for the first time just how badly the damaged wheel canted on its axle. To a question from Darby, the messenger answered gruffly, "Oh, we'll get it fixed, all right. But it's anybody's guess how long it will take. I'd say we'll be doing damn good to have this outfit rolling again by midnight!"

Darby considered this news as he stood and watched the crippled stage being hauled off toward the company yard, where there were men and equipment for making the necessary repairs. The other two disgruntled passengers were moving off together toward the nearest bar to warm themselves and take on fortification against the delay and the chill night ahead. Now he saw Ned Archer leaving the hotel lobby. Archer looked quickly around and, by the glow of an oil lamp burning near the doorway, caught sight of Darby. He hurried down the steps.

"I thought you were right behind me," Archer said. "I was about to check us into a room when I wondered what became of you."

I just bet you did! Frank Darby thought. Archer's assignment was to keep an eye on him; consequently, he was apt to grow uneasy if he happened to let the other man out of his sight.

"It's too early yet to turn in," Darby casually said. "I thought I might stretch my legs a bit first—take some of the kinks out of them. How about joining me?" And as the other man hesitated, he added, "To tell the truth, I have a little proposition I'd like to discuss with you."

Archer looked sharply at him. "What kind of proposition?"

"Oh, a little something I couldn't very well discuss in front of those others."

He could almost see the curiosity he had set working in Ned Archer's mind. After an uncertain glance at the dark street, Archer said, "Well, all right. But not too long. It's chilly for walking."

"Just a block or so, and back."

They started off through the village, a raw place of a couple of hundred people. They passed from darkness in and out of the brief glow of lamplit windows, moving in a stillness that was broken chiefly by the sound of their own footsteps and the whine of a chill wind down from the mountains to the west.

Darby let Archer grow impatient enough to ask finally, "Did you say something about a proposition?"

"Why, yes," he coolly replied. "I did, as a matter of fact. I was wondering if the two of us could hit on a deal. For instance," he went on, unhurried, "how does a thousand dollars sound to you?"

"A thousand—?" Archer halted in his tracks, turning to stare. "I'm afraid," he continued flatly as they started on, "I have no idea what in the world you're talking about."

"I think you do." Darby allowed an edge to creep into his voice. "So let's speak frankly for once. There's not a soul who can hear us or repeat what we say. You know perfectly well why I was sent off to Denver—and *I* know why you've been ordered to come along. It's time we stopped lying to each other."

There wasn't a word from the other man, though Darby thought his breathing suddenly had grown a little ragged. "There's a thousand dollars in my pocket," Darby continued in the same cool tone. "It's yours, in return for one small favor. After we get to Denver, you'll simply become a little careless for something like twenty seconds—believe me, that's all I need. By then I'll be out of sight, and no matter how you hunt, you won't be laying eyes on me again. You'll wait a week, and after that you'll go back to Santa Fe and confess to Tom Hanlon what went wrong. He won't like it, of course. He may come down a little hard on you. But what's a small tongue-lashing, when we're talking about a thousand dollars? And that's what one week's leeway is worth to me. So?" he prodded when he got no answer. "Do we have a deal?"

Archer's continued silent plodding told him the man was preoccupied—and thinking hard. At that, Darby let a contemptuous smile warp his lips, knowing his guess had been right: This incorruptible man Friday of Tom Hanlon's was as open as any other to temptation. You could almost smell the greed working on him.

The toe of Darby's shoe struck something, and slowing his stride, he leaned over and touched it. It was a piece of rock lying in the street, large enough to fit the palm of his hand. He picked it up.

He had dropped back a pace, and now Ned Archer wheeled on him, exclaiming in a harsh whisper, "Damn you, Darby! What are you trying to do to me? The answer is no! *No!*"

Frank Darby struck.

The rock was a hefty one and the blow was solid, but

the victim's hat helped cushion it somewhat. A grunt of pain exploded from Archer and he staggered, the hat dropping from his head. Darby hit him again, and this time he thought he felt the skull give way. Without another sound, Archer went to his knees and then tumbled forward onto his face in the ruts of the street. Standing over him, Darby said aloud, "Fool! Did you really suppose I'd waste a thousand on you? Not even a penny!"

He lifted his head then and looked sharply around him. The night was as black and silent as ever, its stillness broken only by the wash of the wind, and there was the mesh of stars alone for witness. The nearest buildings were dark and seemed to offer no threat of anyone interfering. Still, it was a perilous situation to find himself in, and Darby went quickly into action.

Tossing aside the rock, he leaned to examine his victim. The limpness of the body as he rolled it onto its back told him Archer was dead. He found the fallen hat and dropped it onto the man's chest. Then he caught Archer by the wrists and quickly dragged him out of the street and into the weeds that edged it. Here there was a shallow depression, and he rolled the body into it, knowing it would be hidden there until daylight—plenty of time for his purposes. There was one last detail. Hastily but methodically, he went through Ned Archer's clothing, turning pockets inside out and helping himself to whatever money and valuables he found. When his victim was found, it would be obvious that he had been waylaid and struck down by an assailant bent on simple robbery— probably looking for drinking money.

Darby straightened and stood for a last moment beside the man he had killed, savoring the swift elimination of a vexing problem. Suddenly he was flooded with a rush of confidence and triumph, almost of euphoria.

Frank Darby turned and started through the windy darkness toward the Hanlon wagonyard. By this time, the way his fortunes were running, the damaged wheel would be nearly mended, and the eastbound stagecoach would be ready to carry him on his momentarily interrupted journey. He could imagine nothing else between here and Kansas City to keep him from Beth Hanlon—the woman he loved and intended to have, at any cost and in spite of any obstacle.

Chapter 6

For the passengers on the stage heading toward Santa Fe, this swaying coach with the scenery wheeling monotonously past its windows had become the whole of their universe, in which they hung as though suspended in space and time. After two full days and nights, they had begun to get used to the discomfort and the unbroken routine—stopping for new horses at lonely stations, each as bleak as the next, and enjoying a rare break for meals at the larger home stations. At intervals, a new driver would climb up onto the forward boot and take his place next to Clay Reiner—whom Beth Hanlon increasingly saw as a reassuring presence, always there, always in charge.

Beth had even managed to learn again the knack of sleeping upright, while the stagecoach made its way through the windy darkness. And now, on this third morning, though her fellow passengers were showing the effects of their ordeal, she thought most seemed in better spirits. Perhaps this was because they knew Bent's Old Fort, where they were scheduled to make a noon halt, marked the midpoint of the journey. It helped to think it was almost half over.

Up until now they had ridden in almost complete silence, each with his personal misery. But this morning the atmosphere was a good deal freer and friendlier—all except for Harris McRae, who still hadn't spoken to Beth since their angry exchange the day before. Mary Hanlon and Amelia Winfield soon fell into conversation, and Beth listened with interest to their talk.

"How long have you and Lieutenant Winfield been married?" Mary asked.

"Almost fifteen years now. We were both quite young."

"He's always been in the military?"

"Oh, no," the blond woman said. "Not until the war. He signed up out of patriotism—like everyone else. But it was almost as though he knew at once he'd found the place where he belonged. After the fighting ended, he went back to civilian life, thinking it was what I wanted. But—I don't know, it just never seemed the same. He tried it for a year—photography, even reading for the law. He was very good at all of it. But finally he made up his mind that the service was the only place, after all, where he could do what was right for him."

Beth watched her mother's expression as Mary looked at the woman in earnest puzzlement. "And you didn't mind?"

"I want him doing what makes him happy. I urged him to reenlist." She paused as though seeking the right words to explain. "Naturally, the separations can be lonely for a soldier's family. But it was a part of our plan that, as soon as he got a permanent assignment, Johnny and I would go join him."

"Even at a post somewhere in the middle of nowhere?" Then Mary added, slowly, "You must love him very much. . . ."

The woman's only answer was an agreeing smile, which removed years from her tired features.

Beth looked at her mother and had a sudden understanding of what was troubling Mary Hanlon just now: the contrast between this woman's devotion and her own failed marriage to Tom Hanlon.

Until the long talks they'd had this past summer in Missouri, Beth had never realized the depth of her mother's problem. Mary had felt herself driven from her husband by his neglect—by years of being in competition with a business that had taken all his energies and left her feeling of no importance to him at all. So when her daughter had grown and no longer needed her, Mary had fled at last from a situation she no longer could tolerate. Even now, she had told Beth, Tom probably had no real inkling of just why she had left him. It would never occur to him that he had taken her for granted.

Now, with Tom Hanlon injured and perhaps crippled for life, Beth's mother was going back to him—but under what circumstances! It was enough to wring the heart of an affectionate woman like Beth, who dearly loved both her parents. Could it have been, she wondered, that their marriage was wrong from the beginning?

She shook her head, her lower lip caught between her teeth as she pushed that thought aside. Her parents' love had once been as sure as—why, her love for Frank Darby! Beth recoiled from any suggestion that such an emotion could be an error that would betray one as time passed. Suddenly she felt a tremor of something strangely like fear; she longed for this interminable journey to be over, to be in Santa Fe again and safe in Frank's arms, while he reassured her that these doubts of hers were meaningless. . . .

The valley of the Arkansas River, stretching broad and flat between sandhills on the south and a line of chalk bluffs on the north, was often called the best natural highway in the world. In this arid section of eastern Colorado Territory, it could also be a treacherous one, with thunderstorms or runoff from the snowfields of the Rockies sending flash floods to tear up the land and alter the river's course.

Only last June, such a flood had all but demolished a military post in the Big Timber region. Now Fort Lyon was being rebuilt some twenty miles farther west, near a juncture with the mouth of the Purgatoire River. Here the travellers found men in fatigue uniforms toiling like ants—working with timber and stone and adobe. They had to get as much of the rebuilding done as possible before the fierce, bone-chilling winter settled like an iron lid over these empty eastern Colorado plains. The coach stopped only long enough to drop off a small bag of military mail. After a brief exchange between the driver and the postmaster, the stage was gone again, and the raw, unfinished place was left behind.

Young Johnny Winfield was riding in the forward boot. Clay Reiner, wondering from the boy's expression if he had been dismayed at what he'd seen back there, ventured to comment, "I wouldn't much like to find myself stuck at a post like that one. Of course," he added quickly, "it's nothing at all like Fort Union. You'll see that Union's a fine, big installation—one of the most important in the territories."

He had discovered before this that Johnny had a way of falling silent when the subject of the army was mentioned. This puzzled Reiner, but he had learned to respect the youngster's silences—his sudden shifts from boyish enthusiasm to a moody quietness that wasn't easily breached. He let the talk go for now, but presently he pointed and said, "Look up ahead. Do you see them?"

The boy frowned as he peered toward the far western horizon. "See what? Them clouds, you mean?"

"There's mountains under them. You've come a long way for this. You're looking at the front range of the Rockies!"

It took Johnny a moment to grasp it, and then he seemed disappointed; it was obviously far different from what he had looked forward to.

Reiner smiled slightly. "The mountains are still about a hundred miles away. You wait, though. They're going to get a lot more impressive."

"Will we be going across them?" Johnny's enthusiasm began to increase now.

"Well, not directly. We'll more or less skirt them. After leaving Bent's Fort, we strike southwest along Timpas Creek to Trinidad. Tomorrow we'll cross Raton Pass into New Mexico Territory. But that pass is over seven thousand feet," he added. "I think you'll know you've been in the mountains!"

On only one other point did the boy also seem disappointed. "I was thinking we'd have seen some Indians. . . ."

Reiner couldn't keep a hard edge from his reply. "Don't give up hope. We might yet!"

"Indians on the warpath?" Johnny exclaimed eagerly.

"Let's hope not. We're supposed to be under a treaty of peace. Still, this is Indian country, and you'll likely be seeing some—that is, if they *want* you to see them!"

Reiner abruptly dropped the subject. It wasn't his intention to say anything that could alarm the youngster.

It was a little after noon when the stagecoach approached Bent's Old Fort, the halfway point between Santa Fe and the railhead in Kansas. Thirty-four years earlier, on a gravel bench above the flat river bottoms, Charles and William Bent and their partner, Ceran St. Vrain, had erected this first substantial building of any sort in the territory of Colorado—a fortress where they could carry on trade with the Cheyenne, Arapaho, Apache, Ute, Comanche, and Kiowa. They built it on a huge scale, of the kind of adobe brick they had seen used in Santa Fe. Its walls were fourteen feet high and surrounded a spacious courtyard, which was lined with dwelling and storage rooms and a building to store buffalo hides.

Years later, William Bent, the sole survivor of the original partnership, grew despondent over the changes brought by the forty-niners and by the advent of cholera among the Plains tribes. As though driven by ghosts of the past, he took his Cheyenne wife and children and abandoned his fortress, after first stacking the rooms with kegs of gunpowder and blowing them up.

Now, its walls partially rebuilt and whitewashed and a number of its rooms again made usable, the old fort stood as a landmark on the stage road to Santa Fe. As before, it dominated the flat valley and the shifting course of the Arkansas. And despite its crumbling condition, it was the best-equipped station on the run.

Here tight schedules were somewhat relaxed. Stage passengers were given time for a leisurely meal and even a chance to wash, change their clothes, and make ready for the second half of their journey. Also, this being the midpoint, the coaches that had left the opposite ends of the line a couple of mornings earlier usually met here to compare notes on the route each had covered. Behind schedule himself, Clay Reiner rather expected to find the eastbound stage already arrived. When they rolled into the compound past the wide, iron-studded gates, he was a little surprised to see no sign of the other coach.

The stationmaster's wife, always eager for the sight of another woman, was delighted to see three of them. She greeted them and hustled them off to show them where to clean up before sitting down to the meal that already was cooked and waiting. Reiner stayed behind for a talk with her husband, exchanging news of the journey and of the trail ahead. The man had heard nothing of the eastbound coach, nor word of any danger that might give cause for alarm. But Reiner was uneasy as he left the teams being unhitched and crossed the windswept compound to the room where the rest of the party were already at dinner.

Like the dining rooms of most such stations, this one was largely filled by a long trestle table and benches. Reiner saw at once that the people from the stage were all clustered close at one end; then he saw the reason. A man in the uniform of an enlisted man, with a sergeant major's

68

chevrons on his coat, was holding down the far end of the
table by himself. He had finished his meal and had lit up a
villainous cigar, which could explain why the others were
letting him have that section of the room to himself.
Reiner chose his utensils, filled a plate from the platters of
rough, stage-line fare, poured himself a cup of black coffee, and carried them down to where the noncom sat
enjoying his smoke with arms folded on the edge of the
table.

"Hi, Reiner!" The sergeant's grin, breaking a brick-
red face, showed his big, square teeth clamped on the
stub of cigar. He reached a hamlike fist that engulfed the
newcomer's, as Reiner let himself down onto the bench
across from him. Sergeant Buck Newcome was attached to
one of the companies downriver at Fort Lyon. "Ain't seen
you for a spell," he said genially.

"I come and go," Reiner said as he started to work on
the plate he had piled high. "Haven't been in these parts
lately. We came by the new post," he added. "It looks like
it's beginning to take shape."

Newcome wagged his head with a grimace. "Too slow,"
he said. "Damned slow. We'll never have it done before
the snow hits! That's why the captain sent me over here
this morning. Looks like we may have to winter some of
our men here at the old fort."

"What's been the problem?"

"Same as ever—not enough time. We've only had
since June, when we got flooded out at the old place. And
right now we're below strength from desertions. You can
lay part of the blame on that."

"Is that something new?"

"Naw. It's the same every year. Give those yahoos a
taste of what it's really like on one of these frontier posts,
and a lot of 'em decide it sure as hell ain't how *they* want
to spend a winter. In particular, they figure they don't
want to spend it trying to build the post around them! So

you got to watch them every minute, because somebody's sure to take off whenever your back is turned. It leaves us shorthanded for finishing the work, besides playing hell with my morning reports!"

He looked at the cigar butt, checked the way it was burning, and then shoved it back into the same corner of his mouth, beneath the heavy brush of black mustache. "You're taking this stagecoach through yourself?"

Reiner nodded above the rim of his coffee cup. "Maybe you heard about what happened to my boss."

"Yes, I sure did. Too bad."

"I haven't seen him since the accident, and I thought it was about time I did. Besides, I've got his family with me, and it's my responsibility to get them safely to Santa Fe."

"Well, I'll make a small wager you run into weather before you get across the pass. We're due."

"Maybe it'll hold off," Reiner replied.

"Don't count on it. Take my word—a man that spends time in this Colorado wilderness pretty soon develops a nose you can't beat." He touched his own with a broad finger. "And me, I smell a storm coming!"

"It's something you can always figure on, this time of year. I just hope we don't run into anything worse than weather."

Newcome gave him a shrewd glance. "You're talking about Indian trouble. . . ." He paused, with a quick glance down the table to see if the stage passengers had heard what he said. The sergeant hesitated, scowling. "If you're about done there, maybe we ought to take this talk outside."

Clay Reiner nodded. He finished eating, dropped his silverware onto the plate, and drained off the last of his coffee. The others were talking to the stationmaster's wife, paying them no attention. Reiner and the sergeant got up from the table and strolled out into the bleak sunlight. There, alone in the courtyard where they wouldn't be overheard, Newcome plunged ahead with his sour comments.

"I just don't like the situation. One of the army's main jobs out here has always been to keep the trails open and supply escorts for the stagecoaches and wagon trains that use them. But now, because we got us some names signed to a treaty, I guess *that's* supposed to take care of everything!"

Reiner had taken out his pipe and was shoving rough-cut tobacco into the bowl. He said dryly, "You don't appear to think all our problems were solved at Medicine Lodge. Things *seem* quiet enough."

This drew a snort from the other man. "For how long? Hell, we've had the treaty less than a month! Sure—so far there ain't been any trouble to speak of. We've had patrols out—as many as the old man could spare from building that damn fort. They haven't run into anything. There's some who think the tribes have already gone to their lodges, holed up for a tough winter."

The sergeant pulled the cigar stub from his mouth, spat into the dust, kicked the stain with his toe, then shoved the butt back in his mouth and continued. "What *I* say is just wait till it soaks in on those people that they're supposed to have given up their hunting grounds forever and agreed to let themselves be herded onto reservations! Then we'll see what trouble really looks like! Hell, they'll never admit their chiefs had a right to sign to such a thing. Count on it—one of these days we'll get word that some emigrant wagons have been waylaid and burned, or a stage station sacked, or a coach has arrived stuck full of arrows like a pincushion. That'll be our sign that the Plains tribes have finally caught on to the fine print in that Medicine Lodge treaty! They'll be letting us know just what we can do with it!"

There was no good answer for that. "You could be right," Reiner acknowledged.

Newcome plucked the cigar end from his teeth, decided he had finished with it, and tossed it aside. He

71

squinted at the hang of the winter sun above the western wall of the old fort. "Well," he said, "I'm past due at the post—but I figured I'd use the chance to get some real grub!" He grinned and patted his belly. "I got to make tracks. If I don't see you again right soon, you take care. Hear?"

"Same to you."

Moments later, the sergeant rode away across the compound, his McClellan saddle strapped to a rangy army bay. Reiner stood and watched the man turn at the gateway for a half salute in farewell and then lift into a canter as he passed from sight. Reiner worked at his pipe as he stood contemplating the things they had been talking about. Still frowning in thought, he turned to walk over to where the stagecoach stood waiting for the fresh teams that would take it on.

It was then that he heard another coach arriving. He turned back, and a moment later a stage came swinging in through the gateway. The horses were lathered, as though they had been kept working in the harness. But it looked as though his nagging uneasiness about the delay in the arrival of the stage from Santa Fe was shown to have been unfounded.

The messenger on the box saw him and waved an arm in greeting. As the stage pulled up, hooves and wheels lifting gritty dust for the wind to whip away, Clay Reiner called, "You're a little late, aren't you?"

Alighting, the man explained. "We busted up a wheel coming down from Raton Pass, and it cost us a couple hours at Trinidad getting her fixed. We've been trying ever since to make up what we lost." Otherwise, he reported an uneventful trip—no trouble with the road or the weather and no sign of hostile Indians.

But all at once, Reiner was scarcely listening.

Both doors of the stage had been flung open and a few passengers were getting out. He found himself staring at one of them—the last person he would have expected to see. And as he stood rooted in surprise, he heard Beth Hanlon's exclamation.

"Frank!" she cried as she came hurrying across the compound. And Clay Reiner quickly turned away—unwilling to watch this reunion between the woman he loved and the man she was engaged to marry.

Chapter 7

Beth thought it would be hard to say whether she or Frank Darby was the more startled. He looked at her as though stunned—like a man in shock. His smooth cheeks appeared drained of normal color, and when she seized both his hands in hers, she received at first no answering pressure. He found his voice, and he stammered her name. Then, after a hasty look around, he drew her aside from the activity near the coach. In the compound of the ruined fort, they stood together, oblivious to anything but themselves.

"Beth!" Darby said again, hoarsely. "You're supposed to be in Missouri! What in the world are you doing *here*?"

"I could ask you the same thing." And then she felt herself go cold. "Is there more bad news? Oh, Frank! Is it Pa? Has he—?"

"No, no!" he said quickly, reassuring her. "Tom was doing just fine when I last saw him, the day before I left." Frank's handsome features clouded. "But I gather that you heard about the accident, then."

"Yes, I did. From Clay Reiner."

"Reiner?" He repeated the name with disapproval. "Dammit, he shouldn't have told you! That was directly against Tom's wishes!"

"Pa had no business trying to keep us in the dark," she responded quickly, not sure why she felt she had to defend Clay. "As soon as we heard, Mother and I decided we had to come at once."

"Your mother? Is *she* here, too?"

Nodding, Beth indicated the building she had just left. She explained, "It was all done on the spur of the moment, or I'd have let you know. But a letter wouldn't have reached Santa Fe any quicker than we would ourselves." And then, at something she saw in Frank's eyes and in the set of his mouth, she caught her breath. "Are you *angry* with me?"

"What? No—no, of course not," he told her quickly. "It's just that—well, I simply can't get over running into you like this, in the middle of this wilderness—when I was on my way to Missouri, looking for you."

"Why, then," she said, suddenly smiling, "I've been able to save you some trouble. Now that you've found me, we can all go on to Santa Fe together."

"You don't understand!" he blurted out, in a tone that caused the smile to die on her lips. "I've left Santa Fe for good. I'm never going back there. I can't!"

She stared. "You don't mean this!"

His answer came in a tumbling rush of words that left her deep in bewilderment. "Beth, it's all ended! I've known this was coming. Things just haven't been right. I wasn't getting anywhere, working for your father. It's true!" he went on before she could protest. "We've been arguing constantly—since long before the accident. Arguing about *you*, Beth! Somehow, it entered his head that I had no real interest in you except as a way to shove him aside and take over his business. I hope you know as well as I do—that's utter nonsense!"

"But of course! Where could he have gotten such a notion?"

He shook his head. "Who knows? I suppose a man who's worked as hard as he has, building that stage line, is bound to be protective of it—suspicious of other people's motives. Following the accident I tried to blame it at least in part on the confusion in his mind and all the pain he's suffered. But finally there was a moment when I couldn't take any more. It all came to a head—and I quit my job. Now I won't go back there until I've proven that I can succeed on my own!"

"Oh, Frank!" She felt the sting of tears. Shocked and miserable, she could only protest, "There *must* be something—some way . . ."

"No!" He said it almost fiercely, adding quickly, "Anyhow, we haven't time now to talk about it. See—they're getting your stage ready to leave." He took her arm and turned her toward the activity at the westbound coach, where fresh horses were being brought up. Into her ear, he whispered in earnest petition, "Beth! Don't get on it. Stay here with me!"

"*What?*"

She turned to stare up into his face. Despite the wash of sunlight, the day was chilly—but there was no mistaking the sheen of perspiration she saw at his temples or the tremor in his voice as he said anxiously, "Please, darling— stay and take the other coach east with me. You've *got* to! There are places you've never even heard of. I want you to have them all. And I want to be the one to give them to you! New York, Boston—maybe even London and Paris! They're all waiting! This godforsaken country out here isn't for you—for us!"

Beth wanted to protest, but she was too bewildered and shaken by his persistence. When she found her voice, what she said was, "Frank, don't you see I can't do that? Mother would never understand. And meanwhile, there's Pa—lying there helpless! To have come this far, and then not even to see him—perhaps for a last time. . . ." She clutched at his hand. "Oh, please! Come to Santa Fe with us. I won't insist that you stay. I won't even ask you to face Pa again if you're that set against it. But at least give me a chance to have things out with him. Perhaps I can set the whole matter straight."

"*No!* I tell you, it's hopeless!"

"Nothing's ever hopeless. And if I do fail," she went

on, her eyes on his as she spoke with level earnestness, "I give you my promise: I'll be prepared then to go away with you, any place you say. Only, first—if you really love me—I know you won't refuse me this one thing."

She saw refusal in his scowl and in the stubborn line of his jaw. But he must have seen her own firmness, and it was Darby who in the end gave way. He lifted one shoulder in a shrug. Then the darkness left his features, and suddenly he was smiling in a manner that altered his whole appearance. He sounded no more than a little perturbed as he said, "Very well—even though I can't believe anything will come of this. If that's how you must have it, I'll fetch my belongings from the other coach. Do you suppose there's time to grab myself a bite of something to eat before I begin my journey back to New Mexico?"

As he left her and started across the compound, Darby masked a savage fury. At the last moment, he had realized he must at least appear to agree to Beth's insistent demand. Something had warned him that she wouldn't be swayed from a determination to see her father and that to flatly refuse would be to risk losing her. And that was the one thing he wasn't prepared to do.

Something else was equally certain, of course: Under no circumstances would he let himself be dragged back to Santa Fe to face sure prosecution on a charge of embezzlement! He had to find some way out of this dilemma, and he had only a matter of hours in which to do it. Still, Frank Darby was a man who trusted his wits and his ingenuity. He would find the key. Nothing, and nobody, was going to take Beth Hanlon away from him. . . .

An obscure impulse, born of his talk with Sergeant Newcome and a natural sense of caution, had prompted Clay Reiner to order a horse saddled, now that they would be quitting the valley of the Arkansas River and crossing over into rougher country beyond. Whether or not the risk of danger was any greater, at least he felt more independent. Astride a long-limbed roan, with a Spencer repeating rifle in the saddle boot and his belt gun fully loaded and ready in its holster, he enjoyed the greater mobility after days of inactivity on the driver's seat of a stagecoach. A man often felt like a sitting duck, exposed on that high and swaying forward boot. On horseback, he could range ahead and even leave the road if a need presented itself.

His new driver on leaving Bent's Fort was a lean, black-haired fellow with a reckless manner but a steady hand with the horses. Ernie Shotten was known for having an independent streak, yet Reiner had always found him reliable. They crossed the Arkansas by way of a ford that could offer problems in floodtime, but at this late season— at the tail end of a dry summer and fall—it was manageable enough. Leaving the river put them at once into country that had been Mexican territory back in the days when the Bents set up their trading post on the American side.

With the long front range of the Rockies beginning to loom like a wall, shutting off the western horizon, their route changed and now swung southwest, lifting toward a southern extension of the mountains—the Sangre de Cristos—which they would cross at Raton Pass, coming at last to New Mexico. In between lay an arid land of thin grass and yucca and cactus, breaking up into sandstone mesas capped with limestone—a land of intermittent streams that shrank to nothing except during thunderstorms or the spring flash-flood season.

The cloud sheet that had moved across the wide sky, dulling the day, mirrored the thoughts and feelings troubling Reiner since the sudden arrival of Frank Darby. So far, he hadn't been told a reason for the man's appearance at Bent's Fort, or for his changing his mind and returning with them to Santa Fe. He couldn't even guess what might have passed between Darby and Beth Hanlon, though he suspected it was something that upset her badly. Much as he would have liked to know what was going on, he reminded himself grimly that she wasn't his girl. He would have no business interfering. He just wished he liked Frank Darby a little better!

There was nothing specific about the man, nothing he could put his finger on. Anyway, Reiner suspected it wouldn't have made much difference if Darby had been the most outgoing and likable man he'd ever met. That he was the man Beth had chosen was bound to stand between them—and for that Reiner had to blame himself.

Watching earlier as Darby was introduced to Beth's relatives, he'd seen Mary Hanlon greet him pleasantly enough. But Harris McRae had really let out all the stops. McRae was all too obviously impressed by Darby's style and charm, even before he learned that this was Beth's intended. Clay wasn't sure why he had been so wryly certain those two men would hit it off, but he wasn't surprised when they did. Now he was happy not to have to travel on the same coach as the pair of them—or to be forced to ride in such close proximity to Beth and her betrothed.

They were a couple of hours across the river, with the next swing station a few miles ahead of them, when all other thoughts were jarred out of Reiner by a distant burst of gunfire. Had he not been riding a little way ahead of the coach, the sound might have been missed in the noise of timbers and hoofbeats and the rattle of dry brush moving before a rising wind. But that wind shifted direction slightly, and now the gunfire came more clearly. He drew rein quickly to listen.

Reiner placed it somewhere ahead and to his left. Moments later the coach came abreast of him, and Ernie Shotten pulled in his teams and called down, "What's wrong?" And then he swore as he heard what Reiner had been hearing.

Harris McRae thrust his head through a window to exclaim, "Do I hear guns?"

"Quite a number of them," Reiner replied. It sounded

80

as though someone was in trouble—a matter not to be ignored in this country. He told the driver, "I'm going to take a look."

"Want me to wait for you?"

"No." He waved the coach on. "Keep rolling."

"Whatever you say. But watch yourself!"

Reiner was already kicking his horse into motion. He heard McRae yell something after him but chose to ignore it.

It was hard to make out the extent of the firefight, if that was what it was. As he rode ahead along the stage road, he tried to sort out details without too much success. Though he distinguished the reports of both rifles and smaller weapons, their numbers were difficult to judge. But the skirmish lay somewhere just off to his left, to the east of the road, and presently he pulled the roan in that direction and away from the hard-packed wheel ruts.

The firing had eased off, but as Clay approached a slight rise in the ground, he heard a thin chorus of shouting voices that told him he was getting close. He circled a stone outcrop and the land dipped abruptly. Pulling up near a clump of scrub growth, he eyed the scene below him.

The rough ground sloped away toward a limestone face that lifted dull and gray looking under the leaden sky. In between, the flat ground was broken by a stream bed that might hold pools of water in a wet season, but now showed merely as crumbling banks overhanging a silted and sandy bottom. That dry slash in the earth was the focus of the battle.

Drifts of gunpowder smoke, still being dispersed by the steady ground wind, weren't enough to obscure the scene. He saw the Indians first, which was natural, because of their numbers and activity. They were Arapaho, he thought—close to twenty. On the far bank of the dry watercourse, against the limestone face, they were caught up in a fever of excitement. Some had gathered around their leader, while others raced their ponies back and forth in a seemingly aimless pattern, yelling and brandishing weapons to vent high spirits or perhaps to keep up their fighting courage. Reiner watched for a few minutes, trying to make sense of this behavior; then his glance was drawn to the stream bed between him and the Indians, and he understood.

By contrast, the men there were keeping down and nearly motionless, so that at first he hadn't even noticed them. They were crouched against the bank, hugging it for cover from their enemies but clearly visible to Reiner. With an eyeglass he could have looked right down their necks, but there was no need of a glass to identify the blue coats and britches of cavalry uniforms. There were a half dozen all told, and on one he noticed the yellow leg stripes of an officer or noncom. Somehow they had been brought to this predicament—unmounted, badly outnumbered, and pinned down—while their enemies swarmed on the farther bank and howled for their blood.

It looked as though the soldiers were equipped with nothing more than handguns, while Reiner saw that a number of the Indians boasted repeating rifles. That worsened the odds. Even so, the troopers appeared at the moment to be holding their own. On the dry bank above them, there was the motionless bulk of an Indian pony that apparently had been brought down in a frontal attack. If its rider had been hurt, his friends must have hauled him to safety. Reiner suspected this must have been a sobering lesson, and for now things were at a standoff.

But they wouldn't be for long. Reiner's guess was that these were a bunch of young bucks, reckless and ready for anything as soon as their leaders settled on the next move. They weren't likely to quit until the hated white soldiers were driven into the open and finished off.

Reiner frowned, not knowing what he could do about it. He doubted he had been noticed, with the scrubby growth behind him making a backdrop against which the sharp eyes of the Arapaho likely wouldn't pick him out, even had they been less intent on what was immediately in front of them. He slid his rifle into the open, stepped down, and laid its barrel across the saddle. It would be a long shot across that open slope to the foot of the limestone, and he was no more than an average marksman, especially with an unfamiliar weapon. He would have to wait for developments.

There was new movement. Over a game trail that broke down past the end of the limestone, several horses came pouring, with more of the Indians driving them. A glance showed that the horses were the solid colors favored by the army, and all carried McClellan saddles. That seemed to tell part of the story. By bad luck or poor tactics, this group of cavalrymen had been taken by surprise and lost their mounts. The ones in the stream bed would be the survivors who had managed to make it this far, down the limestone and into the cover of the dry creek. Reiner had gotten here in time to see their last stand.

Suddenly, as though at a signal, some of the Indians fell into a line and without warning drove their ponies straight toward the drop-off of the creek bed. As they came, they yelled and fired their rifles—.50-caliber Spencer repeaters like Reiner's, which probably were taken from the saddles of the captured cavalry horses. There was an immediate response from the troopers, who met the charge with pistol shots across the lip of the creek bank. But the attackers halted just out of pistol range, where they milled their ponies, yelling and taunting their foes and shooting at random.

Reiner thought they were trying to get the white men to waste their lead and powder. The troopers, too, must have thought the same way. There might have been a command to hold off firing until they were offered better targets, because the pistols fell silent. The trapped men were forced to hug what protection they had, while rifle bullets kicked dirt around them.

Then Reiner swore. The attack had been a ruse! Already, while the soldiers were distracted, three more of the braves had swung wide to outflank the enemy. Clearly they intended to lead their animals across the creek bed and take the soldiers from the rear. Just as clearly, with rifle bullets pinning them down, the horse soldiers were unaware of the threat. With no time to think, Reiner swept the Spencer to his shoulder and took aim, holding off the trigger until he felt he had the broad chest of the leading horseman targeted. Praying for a good shot, he squeezed it off.

The rifle stock slammed his shoulder, and after a swift burst of white smoke cleared, he realized the shot had been a lucky one. Just before first pony could make its leap, the buckskin-clad rider was knocked spinning. The animal swerved wildly, braking at the edge of the drop-off and veering aside. Reiner already had another cartridge under the hammer, and he caught the second rider in his sights.

This time there was no real chance to aim. As the trigger bit into his finger, the second pony tossed up its head and took the bullet. With a shrill scream of pain, the animal went barreling into the dirt. Its rider narrowly managed to fling clear and roll to his feet. He looked shaken as he turned and scampered back the way he had come. The one remaining horseman didn't hesitate more than a moment before he pulled his pony around and rode away. The attempt at outflanking the soldiers had ended in fiasco.

Reiner saw heads turning as the besieged troopers looked around, trying to locate the rifleman on the slope behind them. He lifted his rifle and swung it over his head, offering encouragement. The Indians, of course, were also aware of him by now. One or two actually took a shot at him, but the distance was too great for accuracy, even with a Spencer repeater. But though Clay Reiner had broken up that one attempt, the situation of the trapped men remained as desperate as ever.

Then there came a new sound, so startling that for a moment he refused to credit it. He turned to stare. At the head of the rough slope leading down from the stage road, a stagecoach suddenly loomed into view. It came on fast, the four horses scrambling and the spinning wheels bouncing wildly over terrain that wheels had never cut before. Stunned, he saw young Ernie Shotten whipping up his teams, the hair flying wildly around his head when his hat went kiting away on the wind.

"Ernie! You fool—*go back!*" But Reiner's yell was lost in the rattle of hooves, grind of wheels, and slam of timbers. The doomed men already were shouting and waving the coach in. With a groan, Reiner turned and leaped again onto the back of his roan.

Now the stage made a skidding turn to a halt, dust billowing up and the stage swaying on its leather thoroughbraces. The horses stomped and blew and moved around in wild excitement. A door of the coach was flung open as blue-clad troopers came scrambling up the slope, making a frantic dash for this one hope of rescue.

Yonder across the creek bed, Indians were already charging forward, firing and shouting their rage; Reiner almost felt his heart stop at the thought of a bullet finding one of the passengers. One of the troopers—he saw the flash of a corporal's stripes on his coat—yelled his companions on and then, turning, sank to one knee and began coolly emptying his revolver at the enemy bearing toward him. The others had reached the stage, and hands pulled a couple of them inside while the rest went swarming up the vehicle and onto its flat roof.

The corporal, his rearguard action successful, turned to join them. He took no more than a half dozen strides when he jerked convulsively and went down. Ernie Shotten, seeing the man had taken a bullet, could wait no longer. A yell at the frightened horses brought them into the harness. Then the coach was away, cutting back across the slope toward the stage road, while that open door flopped on its hinges and the rescued troopers huddled on the roof and clung desperately to the rail.

As Clay Reiner raced down the hill in pursuit of the fleeing stagecoach, he was struck by the bravery of this corporal who had sacrificed himself to help his comrades escape. Suddenly he realized the soldier wasn't dead! As Clay quickly turned his horse toward where the man was lying, the corporal struggled to his feet, took a step, and almost fell a second time. In the next moment, Reiner reached him. Leaning from the saddle, an arm extended, he shouted, "Grab hold!" The noncom hesitated, staring at the horseman with a face white with fright and bullet shock. Then he reached up and Reiner caught hold, somehow hauling the man up behind him. At once they were on their way, in the wake of the speeding coach.

Chapter 8

Clay Reiner held his breath as he rode, expecting one of the stage horses to take a bullet or lose its footing and pile up on the rough terrain. But their luck held, and the horses kept steadily on. The stage jolted from side to side but stayed upright, and Clay's roan ran strongly under its double burden.

Glancing back, Reiner saw that the Indians had been delayed at the stream bed, which proved too wide for their horses to jump. They had to drop gingerly down the steeply crumbling bank, then scramble up again. Though it wouldn't hold them long, any moment of delay was vital. Reiner knew the quality of the fine horses pulling the Hanlon stage—even with the handicap of a heavy and overloaded stagecoach, the teams under Ernie Shotten's whip should hold their own in a flat-out pursuit if given enough of a lead.

The corporal had an arm clamped around Reiner's waist. Reiner called back, "Are you all right?"

"Thanks to you!" The man's voice sounded tight with pain.

"Hang on! There's a station up ahead. If we make it there, we can hold them off." He got no answer—the wounded man was probably saving his strength.

Minutes later, Reiner saw the stage road sweeping toward them, and breathed easier as the coach fell into it and straightened out. The roan, which had been digging for traction in the loose soil, seemed to spurt ahead as it felt the hard-packed ruts beneath its hooves. Dust raised by the coach wheels enveloped Reiner in a choking fog, then was swept away on the wind.

To the rear, the pursuers were gaining ground. Clay could hear yelling behind him and the occasional report of a gunshot. But he told himself gunplay from the back of a running horse was inaccurate, and tried to pay it no attention. Now a glint of water showed on their right—they were drawing in on Timpas Creek, with a limestone ridge to the east beginning to shape up into a shallow valley. Once, Reiner felt the roan break stride as the injured noncom's weight shifted. He twisted quickly in his saddle, caught a handful of the man's clothing, and hauled him back before he lost his precarious seat. Reiner glimpsed the corporal's sweating face, the mouth agape with pain and effort. For breath-stopping moments, the horse labored—then regained its broken stride. Foam from its nostrils blew back and stung Reiner's cheek.

They ran on, but that near mishap had taken something out of the animal. The coach began to draw away from them. Reiner knew they were falling behind, ever closer to the enraged pursuers screaming at their heels.

Then a curve in the road gave him a glimpse of the thing he had been anxiously waiting for—the buildings and corrals of the stage station. They were as crude as any, but he'd never seen a more welcome sight. The structures were of rock and timber, with a feather of woodsmoke above the mud chimney of the main building and a remuda of team horses moving around in the corral. It was a peaceable enough scene—but the people there were already aware of approaching trouble. Three men had rushed outside, weapons in hand, to watch the stagecoach come tearing in with its burden of blue-clad troopers clinging to its swaying roof, and the horses running flat out under Ernie Shotten's whip.

Then the driver was standing on his brake and hauling at the lines, the horses almost piling in a tangle as they tried to come to a stand. Clay Reiner burst through the scatter of dust and pulled in his own lathered mount. Milt Gentry, the stationmaster, was there to catch the reins as he tossed them down. Afterward, hurriedly dismounting, Reiner turned to catch the wounded noncom and ease him to the ground before he tumbled headlong in the dust.

"The fellow's hurt," he told the station agent. "Help me with him."

"*No!*" The corporal waved him off. The left leg of his trousers was soaked with blood, but once his feet were on the ground he somehow found the strength to stand alone. He began immediately shouting at his men as they tumbled off the coach, ordering them into a skirmish line. Reiner decided it was best to let him alone.

Harris McRae emerged from the stage wild-eyed and pale with fright. Reiner had to shout his name twice before he seemed to hear. "Take care of the women and the boy. Get them inside the station. Hurry, damn you!" Belatedly the man shook himself, nodded, and turned to help the other passengers from the coach. Meanwhile, Reiner snatched the repeating rifle from his saddle holster and turned his attention to the danger bearing down on them.

Ernie Shotten had the rifle from under the driver's seat. The stationmaster and his pair of helpers were likewise equipped. The half-dozen troopers had managed to hang on to their pistols, though their saddle rifles had been lost to the Indians along with their horses. With this odd array of weapons, the defenders hastily fell into position. And as the attacking Indians came pounding up out of the dust, they were met by a ragged volley.

It was still too long a range for the rifles, but the sound of gunfire brought those horsemen plowing abruptly to a stop. The corporal yelled for his men to hold their fire, and as the stink of burnt powder swept away, a certain amount of stillness settled over the scene. Tensely, the station defenders waited. A wind stirred the brush along the nearby creek, picked up a small eddy of dust from the stage road, and whirled it among the Indian ponies, setting them moving restlessly.

"Stand fast!" Clay Reiner warned.

He thought he knew the thoughts of the men they faced. Chasing a fleeing stagecoach would be great sport, in their eyes. But now the chase was halted and the quarry had turned to offer them a fight, and that was a different matter. Their blood might be heated to the pitch of excitement, but they weren't fool enough to charge headlong against a determined enemy, even if they happened to have the numerical advantage.

For some moments—nothing. Then, deliberately, one who seemed to be a leader walked his animal out ahead of the rest and halted it, facing the white men. He lifted his voice above the stir of the wind; it ran thinly across the distance, and they didn't have to understand the language to know he was taunting them. His shout was echoed by the rest in a chorus of jeering laughter, at which one of the troopers swore bitterly and had to be silenced by a sharp word from the corporal. Still crowing, the leader pulled his pony around in a tight circle and at the same time thrust his rifle barrel overhead. He fired, setting off a volley of shots at the low clouds. Then the whole group whirled their ponies and started off the way they had come—not hurrying, and coolly presenting their backs as though daring the white men to fire. The stage road carried them around a bend and out of sight. Their dust settled, and it was almost as though they had never been.

Clay Reiner let out a breath from his cramped lungs and slowly lowered the rifle he had held ready. Around him, the others began to stir from their tense and silent vigil.

"That could have got scary in another minute!" someone said hoarsely.

Milt Gentry, the agent, responded, "How do you know it's over? We never hurt them any. No reason to think they won't be back!"

"Maybe not," Reiner said. "Though we'll keep an eye open. But they rode off looking pretty pleased with themselves. For a bunch of young bucks out to see what hell they could raise, they haven't done too bad—they put the army on the run and made a nice haul in riding stock, complete with saddle guns and gear. They'll have great tales to tell at the campfire tonight. Why should they risk suicide trying to do more?"

Gentry ran a dry palm across his wiry whiskers. "I hope you're right," he said, grounding the wire-wrapped butt of an ancient Sharps rifle. "Personally, I'd like to know what set them off in the first place. Hell, we're supposed to have a treaty with those people!"

Remembering his conversation with Sergeant Newcome, Reiner suggested dryly, "Maybe somebody read them the small print. . . ."

For the time, at least, the danger seemed to be past, though Gentry ordered one of his helpers on lookout to watch for any hint of further trouble. A couple of the troopers had taken hold of their wounded noncom and were hurrying him into the station, where he could be tended to.

Reiner saw Ernie Shotten moving around the coach, checking for damage. He walked over to have a word with his driver. Shotten turned to meet him, dark eyes hooded and bony jaw set—a young fellow who suspected he was in for a tongue-lashing or worse.

Without waiting for his boss to begin, Ernie said, "I know what you're gonna tell me, Clay, and I got it coming! Lost my head, I guess. But when the stage come up onto high ground and I saw that fight going on—well, it looked to me them soldiers only had one hope of being lifted out of there alive. So without really thinking, I just went after them!"

Reiner gave his feelings a moment to settle, then he told the man sternly, "I admit, if I could have gotten my hands on you back there I would have skinned you alive!" He was interrupted by an angry shout and looked around.

Harris McRae came striding toward them. He was dishevelled and still shaken by his wild ride behind the galloping stage horses over uneven and trackless ground. He was distraught, almost incoherent, and he demanded of Reiner, "For the love of God, man! What kind of idiots do you and Tom Hanlon have driving these stages for you?" He shoved a trembling fist under Ernie Shotten's nose, while the young fellow turned slowly crimson under his tirade.

"This fool came within a hair of sacrificing an entire coachload of passengers, all for the sake of a grandstand play! No thanks to him that we didn't all of us end piled up back there—dead!"

Reiner's own anger at the driver had cooled somewhat. When McRae paused for breath, he answered him in clipped and quiet tones. "He got you here in one piece, didn't he? Ernie Shotten is a first-class whip—I don't know of another who can handle a coach and four with more skill."

"That doesn't excuse the risk he took!"

"Ernie saw a situation and did what he thought he had to. The result was that he saved the lives of six men. Aside from a little shaking up, I don't see that *you're* any worse because of it."

"Oh, you don't?" McRae retorted, his cheeks darkening. "Very well, we'll just see what Tom Hanlon has to say. I can assure you nobody's heard the last of this!"

"Your privilege, McRae," Reiner said crisply.

"Damned right it is!" And he heeled about and left them, heading back to the station building.

They watched him a moment in silence. Then Shotten lifted his shoulders and let them fall. All he could say was, "I'm sorry."

Reiner looked at him. Instead of the reprimand he might have given earlier, he spoke the simple truth as he said, "Ernie, I'm just glad it wasn't me that had to make the decision. Your choice turned out to be the right one. Don't let McRae bother you. . . ."

Chapter 9

This way station on Timpas Creek was larger and more solidly constructed than some, having served as a home station before someone thought of restoring Bent's Fort from ruin and turning it into a main stopping point for all travel this side of Santa Fe and Denver. However, when Clay Reiner entered the station's main room, he found it crowded almost to overflowing. He stepped into a hubbub of voices and a blast of heat from a cedar log ablaze in the mud-and-stone fireplace.

Standing near the fire were Harris McRae and Frank Darby, deep in conversation. McRae gestured angrily, and it wasn't hard to guess he was still airing his disapproval over the events of the past hour. Reiner gave those two no more than a glance. He was looking for Beth, but failed to see her or her mother.

He noticed that the five troopers who had escaped on the stage had their attention centered on a half-open door, and Reiner wondered if the corporal was in that room, his wound being tended to. But as he was starting in that direction, he caught sight of Amelia Winfield and her son seated at one end of a trestle table, and he veered toward them.

Johnny Winfield showed few traces just now of the strange and moody silence that had bothered Reiner at the outset of this journey. He couldn't remember seeing him this animated. Face flushed, the boy talked rapidly while his mother sat listening quietly, her hands in her lap. The two looked up as Reiner approached.

He asked in real concern, "How are you both?"

"All in one piece," the blond woman said quickly. She managed an uncertain smile. "That was—exciting, wasn't it?"

"Neither of you was hurt at all? You're sure?"

"Quite sure."

Johnny could hold himself in no longer. "Wasn't it something?" he cried. "What we done to them Indians? The driver, he saw what was going on and he yelled out, 'Everybody hold on to your seats. We're going down there!' Next thing we knew, the horses were galloping flat out and we were getting thrown every which way. Then we turned on a dime and pulled up. And next thing, those soldiers was climbing aboard and we got away from there before those redskins even knew what had happened! I saw what *you* did, too!" the boy told Clay. "To go in and pick up that corporal who got shot—that really took nerve!" His eyes shone with something close to hero worship.

Reiner shook his head. "It wouldn't have been right to leave him, not when he'd stayed behind and risked his own life so the rest could escape." He spoke gruffly, bothered by the youngster's praise—troubled with the thought that Johnny's manic enthusiasm might be the thin edge of hysteria showing itself in the aftermath of danger and fright. He turned to the boy's mother. "I'm real sorry, ma'am, that any of this had to happen. I'm afraid your driver let himself get carried away. Whatever his motives were in saving those soldiers, he simply had no right endangering the lives of everybody on the coach. But at least it seems to have turned out well enough."

"I'm glad he did what he did," Amelia smiled. "It could have been my husband down there, and it's comforting to think people would care enough to help." She shifted on her seat, a bit uncomfortably. "But are you sure it's all over?"

"That's how it looks for now, at least," he said. "I imagine it'd be safe to put that thing away." Reiner indicated what he had noticed in her hand. Amelia glanced down and seemed astonished to discover she still was holding the little pocket gun from her reticule. She gasped and turned rosy.

"Oh, my goodness!" she exclaimed. "I dug this out while they were chasing us—and then completely forgot it!" She hastened to return the weapon to its place in her bag.

Watching her, Reiner sensed again the spirit in this woman that had brought her halfway across a continent and into an untamed land. He didn't doubt for a moment that she would use the gun, without hesitation, if it came to a matter of saving herself or Johnny from harm.

He gave her a nod and an encouraging smile, then turned away—almost to collide with Beth Hanlon, who had come up behind him. Beth drew back quickly, and they faced each other. She had removed her winter coat, and in horror Reiner saw blood on a sleeve of her blouse. It was a numbing blow. "Beth!" he cried hoarsely. "Oh, my God. . . ."

"What?" Baffled, she looked down at herself and apparently was surprised at what she discovered. "You mean—this? I'm not hurt, Clay," she assured him quickly. "Honest! I've been trying to help with that wounded corporal, and I suppose . . . oh, Clay, I'm all *right*, believe me!" And she touched him with a reassuring hand— the one, as it happened, that wore Frank Darby's engagement ring.

He knew she could feel him trembling, while a coldness in his flesh told him that the moment of shock must have drained his cheeks of color. With her gray eyes lifted so near to him, all at once it seemed she surely must be able to see through him—to read the secret he had been trying so long to conceal from her. Furious with himself, he could do no more than shake his head and admit lamely, "You really had me scared there for a minute. I'm glad I was mistaken."

"And you? Are *you* all right?" she demanded. "Nobody I talked to seemed to know, so I decided to find you myself and make sure."

"Oh, I'm fine," he told her hurriedly. "Don't worry about *me*." He broke off then; he had just caught Darby's stare trained on him from across the room. He was sure he had never before surprised a look of such naked anger and dislike. Well, if Beth had been *his* girl, he undoubtedly would have been every bit as jealous as Darby.

He dropped his hand away from hers and then asked roughly, "Where's the corporal? I'd like to see him."

"He's in the other room. Come along." And as she led him toward the door, Reiner thought he could all but feel the pressure of Frank Darby's suspicious stare, following them out of sight.

The room they entered was the stationmaster's own living quarters. The massive bed and the commode and mirror were a matching set, which must have been hauled all the way out here from some big city. All the other furnishings at the station had been made on the premises. The wounded noncom lay on the bed with his head and shoulders propped against pillows. His left boot had been removed and the bloody yellow-striped trouser leg slit back to allow his bullet wound to be worked on by the efficient hands of Cora Gentry, with Mary Hanlon assisting. An oil lamp burned against the growing dusk.

The stationmaster's wife, a dear old friend, greeted Reiner. She was a strong, weather-hardened woman, with a friendly and indomitable spirit. "Oh, here you are, Clay," she called out. "Corporal Early has been asking to meet you."

The man on the bed extended a hand. "I wanted to thank the fellow who saved my scalp for me!"

Reiner was noticeably uncomfortable as he stepped

over to accept the handshake, and gruffly replied, "Don't even talk about it."

"All right, but thanks."

The grip of the corporal's hand was firm and solid. He had the air of a seasoned noncom about him, though it would be hard to judge his exact age. The horns of an untrimmed black mustache framed his mouth. His gaze was direct, yet it held an indefinable hint of what struck Reiner as a strange and brooding moodiness.

Milt Gentry came in then, and there were more introductions. "How's that hole in your leg?" he wanted to know.

The wounded man—his name was Fred Early—assured him, "It could be a lot worse. Your missus did a better job than I would've got from that army butcher at Fort Lyon!"

"The bone wasn't broken," Cora Gentry stated. "He lost quite a lot of blood, though."

"Well, take it easy," the stationmaster urged. "Looks like the thing could be pretty painful. I wouldn't say you're gonna be using it very soon."

"We'll see," Early said with a shrug.

Turning to his wife, Gentry suggested, "All these people could probably use something to eat. That stage is going to be hours off schedule getting to the next meal stop. Why don't you see what you can scare up?"

She agreed, and Mary Hanlon added quickly, "Beth and I will be glad to help." Then the three women left.

"I appreciate you letting me be put in your own bed," the corporal told Gentry. "But I can get up now."

"No hurry. Make yourself comfortable." To Reiner, Gentry added, "I'll be right back. I've got something that may prove useful."

Clay had said nothing during most of this. Alone now, he prompted the other to talk by asking, "So you're from Fort Lyon?"

The corporal hesitated. He seemed reluctant to discuss the matter. "We're what's left of a routine patrol," he said finally, "sent out to check on the Arapaho and the other tribes. We were surprised and jumped while taking a rest break. They killed the lieutenant and the sergeant, then grabbed our mounts and our saddle guns and our gear, which is mainly what they were after. While they were busy rounding up the horses, a few of us managed to get away on foot. We were trying for the stage road, which we knew had to be somewhere west. But the redskins came after us and pinned us down in that creek bed. I don't think any of us would have got out alive, except for you and your stage driver."

"Call it luck," Reiner replied. "We happened to be off schedule, or we wouldn't even have been in the neighborhood." He added, "It does look as though the bunch that jumped you was happy to settle for what scalps and horses they were able to collect. They seem to be letting well enough alone."

A new voice demanded, "So, what happens now?"

Reiner turned. The man in the doorway was one of the soldiers, noticeable among the others because of his size and aggressiveness—he wasn't as big as Nels Bregman, but he was big enough. He had a heavy jaw, which looked swarthy because of a dark shadow of beard no razor could have kept under control, and small but piercing black eyes. He filled the doorway. "Now what?" he repeated. "There's only six of us left, and we got no business cooling our heels in some stage station. We should be on our way back to the post, right now."

"I'm afraid that's not possible," Reiner told him. "There are no horses here for you. All we've got are replacement teams for the stages. Most aren't even saddle broke."

The trooper dismissed that objection with a slicing gesture of one broad palm. "No problem. If they got four legs, the men of this outfit can ride 'em."

"Sorry. We can't spare you any. The stage line needs every head."

The piercing black eyes narrowed. "The army comes first, mister! Looks like we'll just have to help ourselves."

Looking directly at him, Clay Reiner said, "Army or not—don't try it!"

They stared at one another. From the bed, Corporal Early broke the sudden edge of tension by saying sharply, "Lake, there's no need for this kind of talk! Maybe you've forgotten, but one of the main reasons the army's out here is to keep the trails open and protect the stages. We'll never do that by commandeering the stage company's livestock."

Trooper Lake turned his angry stare on the noncom, and for a moment they shared a duel of looks that, to Reiner's eye, held more than a hint of some unspoken conflict. Reiner said, "Though we're low on stock, I imagine we can spare one of your men a horse to take a dispatch and alert the command at Fort Lyon. I'm hoping that when they learn what happened today, they'll decide there's danger enough that our coaches should be put back under military escort. For now, the rest of you can stay here. I'll have Gentry fix up a place for you to sleep in the main room. It will give that hurt leg a little more time. Then, when the eastbound comes through on Monday, you can all ride on to the fort."

It seemed to him a perfectly sensible arrangement, but Clay had the instant impression the other two didn't like it. Trooper Lake, as disgruntled as ever, scowled and blurted out, "I ain't for sending no dispatch. Whatever we do, I say what's left of us should stick together."

Reiner looked at the noncom. "Corporal?"

Early hesitated, then answered with seeming reluctance. "I dunno. I'll have to think about it." Reiner could only leave it at that.

Milt Gentry was back, bringing with him a crude-looking homemade crutch someone had nailed together from scraps of juniper wood, with a handgrip and with a crossbar padded with rags. "I had an idea this was still

101

somewhere around the place," the stationmaster said. "I put it together last year for a stock tender to use after he busted his leg in the corral. Should make it easier for you to maneuver," he told Corporal Early, "while that bullet hole mends."

The injured man thanked him, and when Mary Hanlon came in to announce that food was on the table, he started to lift himself up from the bed, reaching for the crutch. But Gentry snatched it away and set it against the wall, saying, "That's for later. Right now, considering how much blood you lost, I think you should stay easy. Cora will bring you something on a tray."

Before eating, Reiner went outside to check with the guard who was keeping watch as early dusk descended. Night was coming swiftly, behind a cloud sheet that let down a fine, needling rain that could turn to something else if the thermometer dropped much further.

He found the stockman huddled into a poncho, an old Henry rifle underneath it to keep the loads dry. No further sign at all of Indians, the man reported. Reiner considered this, peering off into the darkness where the wind had fallen away to nothing, and the only sound was the sibilance of the rain.

"I don't think they will hit us again," he decided. "Not when they know we're ready for them. But keep a good eye open. I'll tell Gentry to have someone out here pretty quick to relieve you."

In the main room, he found all the company, except for Corporal Early, seated to the rather hearty meal the women had managed to put together. The troopers were clustered at one end of the long table. Beth Hanlon and Frank Darby were seated together, and Beth gave Reiner a quick smile when he took a place opposite. Then her eyes clouded as she looked at her uncle, who was holding forth in a voice that stilled other talk in the crude, low-ceilinged room.

Harris McRae's wrath was now aimed at Shotten, the

driver, who sat by himself and said nothing, though his face showed pale and tight with anger. Coldly, Clay Reiner listened.

"It appears to me," McRae was saying loudly, "some people still don't understand how much was at risk today, and how big a loss it could have been for the man who put this stage line together! What happens to *me*," he added quickly with a self-deprecating gesture, "doesn't count. I'm merely Tom Hanlon's brother-in-law. But here's his wife and his daughter—not to mention the man Beth Hanlon is going to marry, and who'll be expected eventually to carry on the work Tom started." McRae leaned back with a self-satisfied smirk.

"The entire family," he presently went on, staring around the table as if challenging anyone to contradict him, "of one of the richest and most important men on this frontier—and they all could have been lost in a single foolish act of bravado by an underling! It would have been the end of everything that gave point and meaning to Tom Hanlon's life—and to the fortune he worked so hard to accumulate. And you can't expect me to agree that it doesn't matter!"

His sister laid a calming hand on his. "Harris! Please!" she protested in her soft voice. "I do wish you weren't so upset about this! We did come through it safe and sound. None of us was even hurt. And besides, there were other lives that had to be considered."

"I don't agree!" he retorted, jerking his hand away. "It was none of our doing that those people let themselves stumble into a trap. After all, when a man joins the army, what does he expect? The rest of us have to support him and pay his wages. If he should finally be called upon to put his life on the line, he has no business complaining."

This drew a shocked gasp from Mary Hanlon. At the end of the long table, one of the troopers was suddenly on his feet. "You sonofabitch!" he shouted. "You really think you're all that much better than us?"

103

Trooper Lake, cursing, reached up to hook a big hand over the fellow's shoulder and haul him down. For a moment the room seemed to hold its breath. Even thick-skinned Harris McRae seemed to sense that he had said too much. He turned crimson as he looked around at the members of his own party and saw their disapproval. He tried to say something more but only stammered, and with a shrug he subsided. After an embarrassed moment, someone made a comment about the patter of rain striking the dark window, and the incident was passed over. But it left Clay Reiner thoughtfully observing the five uniformed men at the end of the table.

If he were one of them, he too would have been angry at McRae's crass suggestion that they should have been left to their fate. They were scowling now, and Trooper Lake was talking to the others, low-voiced and intent. Reiner watched one of them put a canteen to his mouth for a long swallow, then pass it to his neighbor. Reiner had noticed that canteen going around earlier, and he was pretty sure it contained something stronger than water. It could hardly surprise him that these men would be bracing themselves after the ordeal they had been through that day.

One of Milt Gentry's helpers had finished eating and got up from the table to go relieve the man on guard outside. Reiner, dropping his own utensils onto his plate, called after him, "Get the new teams hitched, will you? We'll be through here and pulling out directly."

"Oh, no!" Johnny Winfield's involuntary cry of dismay expressed what most of the passengers were feeling at the thought of going out into that stormy darkness and climbing aboard the swaying coach again, after such a brief spell of warmth and rest and hot grub.

"I'm sorry," Clay said, "but we've lost far too much time already." He looked at Frank Darby. "What was it like when you crossed Raton Pass coming up?"

"Cold and clear," the man said. "But I imagine it's storming there by this time."

"Exactly. We've still got a schedule to make up, and we can't pick and choose our condition of travel. So let's hurry and finish up here."

Reluctantly, but resigned to the discomforts of a long journey, the passengers began to collect their belongings. Outside, now, could be heard the sounds of horses being run out of the corral. Ernie Shotten hastily pulled a parka over his head and shoulders and grabbed up his rifle to go out and oversee the hitching up.

"Hold it!" someone shouted.

All movement stopped. The people in the way station looked around and saw that the five uniformed men had left their places at the table as though at a prearranged signal, quickly spreading out. And each one held an army revolver leveled in his hand, covering the room.

Chapter 10

Clay Reiner, as much taken by surprise as anyone, started to reach for the gun in his belt holster before he saw that Trooper Lake's own weapon was pointed directly at him. The cold, black eyes fastened on him as though daring him to complete what he had started, and when Reiner held back, the big man nodded with satisfaction.

"That's better!" Lake let his stare rake across all the startled faces confronting him. "Everyone hold right where you are. And don't make any dumb moves, because one move is all any of you is going to get a chance to make. I'm looking at *you*, Reiner!"

Milt Gentry found his tongue. "What do you people think you're up to?" he demanded, almost exploding. He got a hard glance from Trooper Lake.

"Oh, we know what we're up to," the big man said. "First off, we want all your guns." A suggestive tilt of his pistol barrel carried its potent threat. "Reiner, take yours out and put it on the table."

There was no chance to refuse. Inwardly seething and still completely in the dark as to what was going on, Reiner lifted the weapon carefully from its holster, stepped forward, and laid it among the littered remains of the meal. One of the uniformed men had come around the table and at once moved in on Reiner, shoving him back. Of the remaining prisoners, Shotten, the driver, was armed with a belt gun and with the rifle he had started to carry outside with him. Glowering darkly, he handed over both.

The stationmaster opened the skirt of his jacket to show there was no gunbelt strapped around his waist. A quick search proved that neither Darby nor Harris was armed.

Lake seemed satisfied, but one of the others pointed his revolver at Amelia Winfield and said, "Earlier, I seen the lady with a little stingy gun. I think it's in her purse."

"Get it!"

The blond woman, white of face and with a look of angry defiance, watched the man's approach, but must have decided there was no way to hold back. She held out the reticule and the trooper snatched it from her, opened it, and removed the small gun. He snorted contempt, dropped the weapon into his pocket, and tossed the purse back to its owner.

With his prisoners disarmed, Trooper Lake seemed more at ease. He lifted a boot onto the bench and leaned his forearm on it, his gun muzzle casually covering the group that faced him.

Fists clenched, Milt Gentry angrily exclaimed, "*Now* maybe you'll be good enough to tell us what this is all about!"

It was Clay Reiner who answered. "I think some of it, at least, should be plain enough," he said roughly. "There never was any patrol. These are nothing more than a handful of deserters from Fort Lyon. I wondered all along how any properly ordered detachment could have let themselves be surprised by those hostiles and jumped as easily as that."

Trooper Lake was eyeing him fiercely. "So you've figured that out! Well, you're right. The bunch of us got together and decided we'd had enough of this damn country—the army, too! We're on our way to Mexico for the winter."

"Does that include the corporal?"

"Did you think he was different from the rest of us?" the big man sneered. "Hell, he went and got himself crosswise with the commander and ended up on charges.

At the last minute he decided he had no better choice than to throw in with us."

"*Trash!*" The scornful epithet burst from Harris McRae. "This is what we risked all our necks for? Pure trash!"

"Why, you sonofabitch!" their leader grunted, rounding on him.

Reiner cut in, to remind McRae, "They're still human beings. At least, we can try to believe it. . . ." He turned to Lake, demanding sharply, "Just what is it you want from us? Those horses I wouldn't let you have?"

"That was the idea to begin with," the man agreed. "But I think we're about ready to up the ante."

"How do you mean?"

"Why, we was listening to this fellow blow off his mouth a while ago." He indicated the fuming McRae. "According to him, some of these people belong to that stage-line operator you work for. What's his name again?"

Reiner felt a cold chill of premonition as one of the other deserters said, "Hanlon."

"That's the one! From what I've heard, he must about own this territory. And right now we got his whole family with us. His womenfolk, his brother-in-law, and this bright young fella here that's supposed to marry his daughter. All of 'em, on their way to join him."

"What about it?" Reiner demanded, certain that he already had guessed.

"Why, *this* about it." Lake's grin suggested he was enjoying himself. "Hanlon being so well heeled and all, seems like he'd figure it worth something to have his family protected. I mean, lots of bad things could happen 'twixt here and Santa Fe, yonder. You seen the proof just this afternoon! But since we was heading that direction anyhow, no reason we shouldn't just pitch in and make sure they're delivered safe and sound. The old man really should appreciate that—appreciate it enough, in fact, to have us on easy street down there in Mexico."

Harris McRae cried indignantly, "We need no help from the likes of you!"

Reiner shook his head in exasperation. "Don't you get it even yet?" he snapped. "The man's talking ransom!"

"*Ransom?*"

"Of course—as in kidnapping. . . ."

Someone in the room gasped. Lake scornfully told McRae, whose face all at once had drained of color, "I guess you need to have everything spelled out for you! All right." He laid out his demands then, in short order, while his followers watched the prisoners like wolves. "We'll be taking the coach. We'll take Hanlon's people, including this one that likes to talk so much—he can be useful delivering our terms to Hanlon and fetching back the cash. The other woman and her kid—" he indicated the Winfields "—they'd only get in the way. We'll leave them here. But we'll need the driver. And finally, mister," and he looked squarely at Reiner, "we'll need *you*— to get us past the stations down the line and order up fresh teams and grub for us when they're wanted."

"You're crazy!" Reiner gritted. "The lot of you! You must have built this scheme out of whatever's in that canteen you've been passing back and forth. Because if you were sober, you'd see it's a proposition you could never get to work."

"Oh?" The man seemed not at all impressed. "Is someone going to spoil it for us? You, maybe?" The black eyes drilled into Reiner. "You better think about that again! I don't think you'd want to see anybody get hurt— the girl for instance." The steely look darted from Reiner to Beth and back again, and the hard mouth quirked. "The first time you try not following orders, something very bad just might happen to her. You get my drift?"

Clay Reiner did, and it was a blow that nearly stopped his breathing. While he kept silent, unable to find a reply to that naked threat, Frank Darby apparently decided it was time to have a word. With studied coolness he told their captors, "You're wasting your time if you suppose you'll be able to get a dime out of Hanlon. You obviously didn't know he's had a bad accident recently. He's still in a coma; nobody's been able to rouse him."

Reiner looked at the man, astonished at the smoothness with which he told his lie. But Lake showed little concern over what he had heard. His lips spread in a knowing grin. "Well, now," he said, his black stare mocking Darby. "That's sort of funny. I've been listening to talk this afternoon about that accident. I didn't hear no mention of any coma. In fact, I got the impression it's all they can do to keep the old man in bed!" Abruptly his manner changed, turning hard and businesslike. "We've had enough jawboning. The ones I said are to stay—step aside." He gestured with his gun barrel. "The rest of us are going to move out. Now!"

"I don't think you are!" a new voice said.

Trooper Lake's head-jerked around. Suddenly everyone was staring at the bedroom doorway, where Corporal Early stood propped on the homemade crutch Milt Gentry had provided for him. The crutch was under his left armpit, supporting his weight. His face, weathered from tough years of army service, looked tight and drained of color.

Lake eyed him coldly. "I think you better stay out of this. While you been lying in there, the rest of us have gone and worked something up. If you want in on the payoff, you'll keep hands off and let us finish what we've started."

"I heard what you're up to." Early sent a scathing look at the other deserters. "You damn fools!" he told them. "What you've started will most likely finish us! Do you really suppose you can get away with stealing a whole coachload of people? Or hold an entire stage line hostage? I credited you with a few more brains than that!"

"Just shut up, damn you!"

The corporal had no intention of shutting up. "I wonder if it's even occurred to you that these are the same people who saved our hides for us today? Or would it matter?"

"Not a hell of a lot," the man retorted. "Not when I figure what we can get for them. It ain't as if we meant to hurt them any—at least so long as they behave themselves. . . ."

Corporal Early shifted position slightly and winced as some of his weight came on the bullet-skewered leg. But his look held firm on the man who confronted him. When he spoke again, his voice was steady enough, though tight with pain. "I ain't too proud of myself," he said slowly. "It's a poor business when a soldier deserts his post. I had the most to lose, which makes me worse than the rest of you. But it doesn't mean I'll stand by and see this go any further."

"No?" Lake's mouth twisted with sudden hatred. "Hell, I knew I never did like noncoms. I've taken the last I'm going to take off of *you*—you sonofabitch!" And the gun in his fist leaped up.

The corporal's right hand jerked into view. He had been holding his own revolver all along, out of sight behind his leg. But he never had a chance to use it. Lake fired twice, the shots deafening in that enclosed space. Pivoting on the crutch propped under his arm, Corporal Early was swung around by the impact of the bullets. He struck the edge of the doorway and dropped.

Everyone, the deserters and their prisoners alike, seemed stunned by the killing. Clay Reiner, with the most riding on his shoulders, was the first to recover. He glanced to his side and saw the uniformed trooper next to him staring blankly at the dead man—for the moment, apparently off guard. Reiner moved almost without thinking, lunging at the man and reaching for the gun he held.

At the last moment, the trooper reacted and jerked his gun hand away. Reiner struck the fellow's arm instead, and the next moment drove headlong into him. The revolver popped from the man's fingers and went spinning end over end as the man was knocked off his feet. Reiner caught himself to avoid falling on top of him. He'd missed his try at the pistol, but his own revolver lay on the table almost within reach. He never hesitated. With two long strides he covered the distance and snatched the weapon up, instinctively sinking to one knee to make a smaller target of himself.

Trooper Lake, standing over the man he had killed, seemed slow to realize what was going on behind him. Not so with some of the others. Reiner saw a revolver muzzle swinging toward him and, propping his wrist upon the edge of the table, got off a hasty shot. It was really too short a range to miss. Through the spurt of smoke, he saw the deserter driven backward and off his feet. Cora Gentry gave a shrill shriek as he almost fell on top of her, while her husband, with real presence of mind, bent to snatch up the gun the man had lost as he went down.

There was an angry shout. Reiner turned and saw one of the deserters shoving people out of his way in an effort to reach the point of disturbance. As the man passed Ernie Shotten, the stage driver suddenly reached from behind, wrapped long arms around him, and threw him off his feet. And when Trooper Lake, with his smoking gun in hand, belatedly swung around to see what was happening, Reiner sent him a sharp warning: "Lake! I'm giving you one chance to throw down your weapon!"

The tables had been turned with blinding speed. Lake and the one other trooper still on his feet had no choice but to get rid of their guns. The whole thing was over even before the door was flung open and the two stock handlers rushed in to see what all the shooting had been about.

The man Reiner shot was clearly dead. Clay's first thought was for the corporal, hoping there might be a chance for him, but when he went to check, he saw at a glance there was nothing to be done.

Gentry came up beside him and said heavily, "It may be just as well for him—the trouble he got himself into!"

Reiner drew a breath. "I'm damned sorry. It looked to me that Early had the earmarks of a good noncom and a proud man. Too proud for his own good, maybe. Probably nobody will ever know what torment he went through to make him desert and go over the hill with scum like these others!"

Reiner had another concern: his passengers. They had seen men killed before their eyes—one by Reiner himself—and they appeared stunned. Beth Hanlon, with a protective arm around her mother, managed a smile for him. He went to Amelia Winfield to return the gun the deserters had taken from her. Young Johnny was completely subdued, his eyes dark against a face drained of color.

"Are the two of you all right?" Reiner asked. He got a quick and reassuring nod—he had known all along this woman possessed resilience and strength beyond the ordinary.

Looking around at the group, he said earnestly, "This has been a bad time, for all of us. I'd have given anything to keep it from happening. Now that it's over, we'll just have to try and put it behind us. All I can tell you is that I'm sorry."

"For what?" Beth said. "It was no fault of yours, Clay."

He glanced at Harris McRae, half expecting some caustic word of criticism, but for once the man had nothing to say. He appeared withdrawn, and Reiner wondered if it meant McRae was aware it had been his own bragging about a family connection with the Hanlon Stage Line that had put ideas of kidnapping and ransom into the deserters' heads and led them all into peril.

Frank Darby alone seemed wholly unperturbed by what had happened. Reiner considered him a moment, wondering just how well he knew this man Beth was pledged to marry. There was something unnatural about such coolness. It made him wonder if anything at all could break past the fellow's controls or upset him. . . .

Milt Gentry broke in on his thoughts and indicated the remaining quartet of deserters standing glumly under the guns of their captors. "Any suggestions what we ought to do with these?"

Reiner considered for a moment. "That's a pretty stout tack shed you've got out back, with a solid door and padlock. Seems like a sound place to stow them, until somebody from the fort can collect them."

Trooper Lake only scowled at him. It was one of the others who exclaimed, "Damn you, it's gonna be a cold night! You can't put us in no shed! D'you want us to freeze?"

Reiner looked at the man. "We'll throw you in some blankets. You can rough it out." The fellow swore at him.

Gentry said, "I'll find a place for these two bodies— let the authorities decide what to do with them. Sooner we can get word to Fort Lyon, the better."

Bert Collins, one of the stockmen, volunteered. "I'll saddle up now and take off for there."

"If you do," Reiner warned sternly, "you ride careful! Don't forget, there are hostiles somewhere between here and the fort."

"Don't worry," Gentry reassured. "Bert's a good man. He'll make it."

"What about the stage? Is it ready?"

"Hitched up and set to roll," the stockman replied.

"Then we've nothing at all to keep us," Reiner pronounced. "Once these deserters have been put safely away, we'll get loaded and hit the road again."

Chapter 11

For Clay Reiner's passengers in the bouncing, cramped stage, the rest of the night was a numbing ordeal—huddled for warmth into the blankets and robes supplied by the stage line, emotions drained and nerves too taut for anything more than fitful sleep. At some hour deep in the night, they pulled into another of the drab way stations, and here Reiner climbed off the box and spoke to the huddled shapes within.

"Anybody want something to eat? Normally this would be our meal stop, if we hadn't been thrown so far off schedule. It will be a good many hours before the next one, and maybe you all ought to have something to tide you over. Some hot coffee, at least."

Harris McRae stirred and groaned. "Oh, God, yes!"

Reiner flipped the iron step into place, opened the door, and left them. Moving stiffly, McRae climbed out. He offered Amelia Winfield his hand. "May I help you, my dear?" he gushed, and she seemed willing for once to accept his fawning attention, taking his arm while he walked her across to the sod building whose lamplit windows suggested warmth and hot food.

The others were also of a mind to take advantage of the opportunity. Frank Darby was next to alight. As Johnny Winfield followed him, Darby said pleasantly to the boy, "You coming too, Johnny? A little something inside us should do us all good!" But the boy only gave him a cold stare before turning to follow his mother and McRae.

The glow of the coach lamp had shown Darby the expression on Johnny's face, and he stared after the youngster with narrow eyes. Now, there was a hard one to crack! Darby had been taking special pains to make himself agreeable to Johnny Winfield, irked by the challenge of someone he couldn't win over. Somehow the youngster's cool-eyed dislike reminded him of Tom Hanlon's housekeeper, Serafina—another person he could never manage to get around, in spite of his every effort to ingratiate himself.

The hell with them both!

He dismissed these thoughts with a shrug, and put on his warmest smile as he turned to help Mary Hanlon down from the coach. Last to emerge was Beth. He had been waiting for this moment. Now, with no one to overhear or interfere, he halted the young woman to ask, "May I talk to you a moment?"

"Why, certainly, Frank," she said at once. "What about?"

"About us, of course. Do you realize we've scarcely had a chance to be alone, even for a moment?"

Nodding, she gave his hand a squeeze. "I know. But under the circumstances—traveling like this—I'm afraid it can't be helped."

"Obviously. Nevertheless, I don't have to like it."

"We both have to be patient. It will be different soon."

"Are you sure?" He looked at her; even now, wan and rumpled in the poor light of the coach lamp, she had never seemed more desirable. He plunged ahead with the line of argument he had been rehearsing. "Beth, do you really love me?"

She stared. "Why, Frank!" she exclaimed at last. "What kind of question is that? Would we be engaged to marry, if I didn't?"

"I'm starting to wonder," he said gruffly. "You seem—changed, somehow. I'm beginning to think perhaps I was

118

wrong to let you leave and stay away from me for almost half a year!"

Beth slowly shook her head, as though in puzzlement. "But you know I only went because I had to—to see my mother. It was nothing to do with you. And as far as I'm concerned, nothing at all has changed."

"You have no doubts of that? I just wish *I* didn't. I seem to have nothing but doubts!" He paused and then played the trump card he had been carefully leading to. "But there's one way you could remove them—that is, if you really care at all how I feel."

"What is it you want, Frank?" She seemed sincerely troubled, studying his face in the fitful glow of the oil lamp.

He drew a breath, and plunged ahead. "Beth, in a matter of hours we'll be in Trinidad, and it's started me thinking. I've heard they have a preacher now. It would only take a matter of minutes for us to call on him—and find out just how serious you are about me!" He adopted his most winning smile.

"You mean, you want us to be *married* in Trinidad?" she asked incredulously.

"Why not?" he demanded. He seized both her hands, eager to convince and persuade her. "We don't have to say a word to your mother or your uncle—either one. We'll just *do* it! After all, this is only between the two of us."

"But—I'm afraid it *isn't*!" she cried. Suddenly her eyes shone with tears. "Oh, please, Frank! It's not all that much farther to Santa Fe. If you don't want a big wedding, it's perfectly all right. But you must understand what it would mean to my folks if we did this to them—on top of everything else! I'm the only daughter they have, and this may be the last gift from me that they can share together."

"What if I were to insist?"

For a long moment, a silence hung between them. Then she slowly shook her head, and when she answered her voice held a new note—unhappy, yet determined. "Please don't, Frank."

Darby dropped her hands, silently studying her. He had a sense, almost, of a door that had closed. He asked himself if he had overplayed it—pressed too hard and perhaps raised a beginning of doubt in her mind. Suddenly he didn't trust himself to speak—a rare experience with Frank Darby. "All right," he muttered. "Let's forget it." And he abruptly turned his back.

Behind him he heard her exclaim, "Try not to be angry!" He shook his head but wouldn't look at her and, after a moment, heard her moving slowly away toward the station. His hands were clenched until the fingernails dug into his palms.

Frank Darby was at an impasse. By his thinking, this had been a logical, if desperate, last attempt. If Beth had agreed—if he had been able to take her to Santa Fe as his wife—surely Tom Hanlon would have been forestalled. But now, with Beth's refusal, his cause looked irretrievably lost. Normally at this point he would have shrugged and cut his losses, walking away from a situation that promised little but disaster. But this time, there was an element he had never reckoned with. This time there was Beth!

Hopelessly enmeshed in his obsession, Darby knew he could only go blindly forward, counting on his wits and on the lucky break that usually came, at a crucial moment, to clear the way to whatever prize he had at stake. Giving up was out of the question. Somehow he would see it successfully through.

So he turned again toward the station, in time to see the door open and two people silhouetted against the light in what appeared to be earnest conversation. They went in and the door closed, but not before he identified them— Beth and that sonofabitch Reiner!

Each time he saw the pair of them together, it irritated him further. He wasn't blind. He had known perfectly well that the fellow would have been a rival for Tom Hanlon's daughter if he could. It made perfect sense to believe that he'd use any opportunity during this journey together to make time with her. All at once the thought sank home: *Reiner just might be doing too damned well!*

Darby hadn't failed to see Beth's undisguised concern for the man during that flurry with the Indians. But what if it went deeper than that? What if it was really Clay Reiner she'd been thinking of just now when she refused his suggestion of marriage at Trinidad!

The startling thought brought a quick intake of air through suddenly clenched teeth. As though of its own volition, his hand came up, pushed aside the skirt of his coat, and tightened on the revolver behind his belt. The weapon had belonged to one of the deserters, and Darby had managed to get hold of it in the confusion following their capture. Now, as he touched the trigger and stared coolly at the lights of the station where he had seen Clay Reiner enter with Beth, Frank Darby began to think that he might yet find an opportunity, and a reason, for using it.

Milt Gentry was an early starter. It was still pitch dark when he rolled out of bed at the Timpas Creek way station, dressed, and got the morning fires going so Cora could begin breakfast. Later, their meal eaten, he and his wife and Ed Jones, the stock handler, pitched into their chores while a gray and bone-chilling dawn was just beginning to break.

Jones went to look at the horses in the pen, and Gentry carried a steaming coffeepot and platter of beans and biscuits to his prisoners in the tack shed. The sky appeared sullen now, under heavy clouds tinged with angry red where the sun was trying to break through. Gentry's breath hung before his face, and the bare ground was frozen to iron under his boots. He didn't envy the deserters their night spent in that shed, despite the blankets they had been supplied with.

He sang out and was answered by groans and curses as the quartet of prisoners stirred and began to move about. Gentry set down his burden and gave a warning: "All of you—stay back from the door!" He used the key in the padlock, removed the chain from the hasp, and drew his gun as he pulled the door open.

Four pale blobs of faces peered at him from back in the shadowed interior. Someone said angrily, "We damn near froze in here!"

"Here's something to help warm you up," Gentry told him. He nudged the iron coffeepot inside the door, and reached for the platter of beans.

It was a dangerous error on his part—the last he would ever get to make.

Too late he heard the quick scrape of a boot on the dirt floor of the shed. He swung around and lifted the gun—in time to have the contents of the coffeepot flung full in his face. Blinded by scalding liquid, he staggered back, crying out in agony. And then they were on him. As he dropped under the rush of bodies, the unfired gun was wrested from his fingers and its barrel struck his skull with smashing force. He never knew anything else.

Trooper Lake grunted with satisfaction. "That does for *him!*" He straightened, holding the captured weapon and looking quickly around in the growing daylight.

One of the others exclaimed, "Watch it!"

"I see him!"

Over at the corral, Ed Jones had heard something that alarmed him. He took several steps in their direction and halted, calling out uncertainly, "Hey! What's going on over there?"

Lake motioned his companions back into the shed and then crouched lower in the doorway, Gentry's body at his feet and the captured gun ready. He waited, and so did the stockman, who was only dimly visible in the deceptive half-light.

Jones was growing alarmed. He said anxiously, "Milt?" And he came on.

Trooper Lake let him, staying motionless until he had a sure target. The stock handler stopped again, not liking the situation. That was when Lake fired. The shot cracked thinly in the still morning. Making certain, he fired again and saw his man spin and drop. Over at the corral, startled horses squealed and stirred.

"One of you," Lake ordered tersely, "see if he had a gun." With the remaining pair, he started at a quick run toward the station building.

They weren't far from the rear door when it was suddenly flung open, letting out a shaft of lamplight. Cora Gentry stood in the opening with a rifle gripped in both hands. She must have heard enough to warn her what was happening. Now, as she saw the blue-clad men rushing toward her, she didn't hesitate; knowing exactly how to handle such a weapon, she snapped it to her shoulder and fired at the oncoming men. She was too hasty. Lake, in the fore, winced at the spurt of muzzle flame almost in his face, but the rifle bullet missed. Next instant he fired, deliberately, and the woman in front of him let the weapon clatter to the ground as she was hit. She struck the edge of the door and slid limply down it.

Lake walked up to her and without compunction prodded the dead woman with the toe of his boot. "Bitch!" he said, without feeling. He stepped over her body, and the others followed him into the building.

A quick look around the station satisfied him they were now in complete command of things. The fourth man hurried in carrying the gun he had taken off the body of the stock handler. Someone said, "Now what?"

"Let's not waste time," Lake said. "We need guns and ammo, and grub to take along with us. See what kind of clothes you can scare up so we can get rid of these damn things." He indicated the uniforms, which would be a dead giveaway wherever they were seen in them. He added crisply, "Now get at it, while I have a look at those horses. That stage has got a lot of hours on us."

One of the men exclaimed, "You still thinking of trying to take it?"

"Hell, yes! Riding light and picking up new animals along the way, we should make a lot better time than any stagecoach. Take my word for it—somewhere between here and Santa Fe we'll run 'em to earth. When I set my sights on a thing," Trooper Lake asserted grimly, "they'll find out I don't let it get away from me this easy. . . ."

Despite the best efforts of Ernie Shotten and of the driver who later replaced him, the coach for Santa Fe was still running woefully behind schedule when it descended, at last, into the valley of the river called the Purgatoire. Here the nature of the land changed, with the Sangre de Cristos close at hand and Fisher's Peak lifting to the south and east. And here, following the west bank of the river, they arrived at Trinidad in late morning, pulling up before the Colorado Hotel.

A chill and boisterous wind pummelled the street and the unpainted buildings. Nevertheless, a number of curious citizens were on hand to see the stage arrive at this unexpected hour and the weary passengers alight. A pair of townsmen came down the steps from the hotel and approached Reiner, Frank Darby, and Beth Hanlon. One was a lean figure with a shock of iron-gray hair, who had a marshal's badge pinned to his canvas coat. After an exchange of greetings, the lawman said, "What happened, Reiner? You're hours late."

"We're aware of that." Reiner told something of their brush with the Arapaho, knowing it would be of prime interest to dwellers in this dangerous country along the Purgatoire. "It could be a signal the Plains tribes are already fed up with their treaty, or maybe only some young bucks on their own, kicking up a little hell. I imagine we will be finding out."

"I imagine," Marshal Corbin said soberly. "Right now, I'm afraid there's more than one kind of bad news for the stage company."

"What do you mean?" Reiner said quickly. "Have you had some report on Tom Hanlon?"

"No, no. Nothing new on him. But—didn't he have a man working for him, name of Archer?"

"Ned Archer? Sure. He's been Tom Hanlon's personal secretary for longer than anyone remembers."

"He ain't no more. Right now, Archer's lying in the back room over at the furniture store. At least that's our identification, from the luggage he left at the hotel. I'd appreciate you having a look to make it definite."

Clay Reiner could hardly believe his ears. "What in the world happened?"

"He was found yesterday morning up the street, lying out in the weeds. Looked like his head had been bashed in with a rock. His pockets were stripped and turned inside out. We figure whoever killed him done it for drinking money!"

Reiner swore, abashed at this news. Ned Archer had always struck him as an officious sort, but a hard worker—and loyal to a fault where his duty to Tom Hanlon and the stage line was concerned. He had deserved better than this.

The marshal's companion was peering at Frank Darby, who had been standing with Beth, listening to this in silence. Now the man said suddenly, "Mister, I'd swear I seen you here in town, night before last. Seems to me you and this dead man—this fellow Archer—got off the east-bound together."

As they all turned, Darby nodded. "That's right, as a matter of fact we did," he agreed promptly. "He and I came up on the same stage from Santa Fe. He said he had business to take care of in Denver. He was planning to lay over and catch the Denver stage in the morning. We had a little stroll up the street and back, stretching our legs. Then we said good night, and a little later I was on my way east again. Archer was alive and well the last I saw of him."

Poor Ned Archer! Reiner thought. Everything indicated that his had indeed been the casual, violent sort of ending that came to far too many in these untamed frontier towns. He lifted his shoulders. "Well," he told Darby gruffly, "if Beth will excuse us, I guess you and I better have a look at him so the marshal can close the books on Ned. If in fact that's who it is. . . ."

And it was. Reiner and Darby stood in the cluttered rear room of the furniture store as Marshal Corbin withdrew the sheet from the face of the dead man; they both silently nodded. Archer, though a fussy kind of fellow, had never harmed anyone, and his loss would hit Tom Hanlon a cruel blow. He left no family, so Reiner told the marshal he might as well be buried in the local graveyard. Later, Tom might have other ideas.

A serious mood still lay on Clay Reiner as they hauled out of Trinidad and presently began the climb toward the pass that was the gateway to New Mexico Territory. On leaving the Purgatoire, following up the course of Raton Creek, they reached dramatically different country, which rose by steep grades into ledges and cliffs that were spotted with juniper and oak and pine. The wind had fallen off, but a cloud ceiling hung low, obscuring the higher reaches of the basaltic mesa that they must cross.

Johnny Winfield was once more in his favorite place, on the driver's seat, and he had many eager questions about this rugged hill country that he finally was seeing. The current driver, Tug Morley, told him stories about old Uncle Dick Wootton, pioneer and friend of the fabulous Kit Carson, who had built this road they were travelling and whose tollgate and roadhouse lay ahead, near the summit of the pass. Reiner took his mind off the murder of Ned Archer by listening to their talk, aware again of the changes he had seen in the boy during these past few days—Johnny had largely shed his moodiness and become genuinely outgoing, while the recent dangers he had undergone seemed to have had no detrimental effects.

In a lull in the talk, as the teams shouldered into their harness and the coach made its careful way over the climbing twists and turns of the crude roadway, Clay commented, "It's the last leg, Johnny. You've had a long trip and a pretty rough one, but in a matter of hours you'll be at Fort Union. I'll bet you're getting excited about seeing your pa again, right?"

The effect on the boy was alarming. His expression changed and the smile left his face, which became a mask as he stared straight ahead of him, not answering Reiner's question. The latter observed him sharply, seeing a return of those troubling earlier silences. For once he was determined not to let Johnny withdraw. "What's wrong, boy?" he demanded. "Just what is it about your father that you don't seem to like to talk about?"

Still no answer, though he could see how the youngster's hands, chafed by the weather, drew up tightly into fists. Then, abruptly, Johnny blurted in a muffled and anguished voice, "Why'd he do it, Mr. Reiner?"

"Do what, Johnny?" he prompted gently.

The youngster turned to him, and suddenly the words were pouring out—things that had been shut inside far too long. "He was a hero during the war. There were medals and field promotions, and once he even shook hands with President Lincoln himself. Then all of a sudden the fighting was over, and it didn't matter what became of my pa. He wasn't a colonel anymore—just a second lieutenant again, the way he started. All those great things he'd done—nobody even cared!"

Clay thought he began to see the boy's problem. He spoke quietly, choosing his words. "But there's always a letdown after a long war. Heroism sort of goes out of style. As for his loss of rank—well, you're an army youngster, Johnny. You know that brevet ratings are only meant to be temporary."

Johnny made an angry gesture. "Sure, I know. That's not the point."

"Then what is?"

The boy hesitated. He obviously was struggling with feelings he had been unable to express for years. "Mr. Reiner, what I don't understand is—why would he go back? Didn't he have any *pride*? It's like he told the army, 'Go ahead! Bust me! Any darn thing you want to do, any old corner you want to kick me into—it's all right, I don't mind!' My pa should be a bigger man than that! I—I don't know how I'll keep from letting him see how *ashamed* it makes me! I plain don't know what to do!" His voice trembled and broke, as though he was on the verge of tears.

Reiner hesitated. He knew whatever answer he made would hold great importance. Johnny Winfield seemed to need a hero. Disappointed with his father, he had increasingly let his admiration attach itself to Clay Reiner, starting with the incident with the drunken stock handler, Nels Bregman, and coming to a head during the encounter yesterday with the deserters from Fort Lyon. Just now he badly needed help. As so often happened with youngsters, he had been nursing a problem created by himself, giving no hint to his mother or anyone else how deeply disturbed he really was. But now he wanted whatever Clay could give, and it was a troublesome question knowing just what to say.

Clay drew a breath and tried. "It doesn't seem to me you have call to be ashamed—far from it! Everything I've heard tells me that John Winfield must be a considerable man, both in war and in peace. And you know, it isn't as though he went back to the army because he'd failed everywhere else. Your mother told me the other day that he did well with every civilian field he tackled, but none of them satisfied him. And so he went back into the service—knowing he'd be starting over with mighty slow chances of advancement in peacetime. Why did he do it? Obviously because he figured that's where his real job lay!"

Johnny had been looking down at his feet, but now his head slowly lifted. A thoughtful gaze met Reiner's as Clay continued, in the same quiet tone, "The war may be over, but out here in the territories the army needs good men—men of John Winfield's caliber—to help make up for all those others who can't take the pressures and maybe turn bad, like that bunch of deserters we ran up against! Johnny," he added, "do you understand at all what I'm trying to say to you?"

Again, a long silence. Waiting, Reiner felt the sting of cold wetness against his cheek; the wind had risen, and the first white streaks of snow were riding it down from the hovering clouds that lay close upon the mountains.

"I guess," Johnny muttered.

"Good! Then just remember this: Any man worth his salt—like your father—is always searching for a job that needs doing, the one that he can do best. If he should be lucky enough to find it, that's reward enough in itself. For instance, there was need of a stage line to Santa Fe—and so my boss, Tom Hanlon, went to work and built one. I've helped him all I could. Right now they're starting to lay a railroad clear across the continent to California. But we can't worry about that! For the time being the stages are still needed, and as long as they are, keeping them running will be our job. If in a few years a railroad puts us out of business, then'll be time to look around for another job that needs doing. And it's exactly the same with your pa and the army, now that the war is over. You might think about that some, Johnny."

His only answer was an almost imperceptible nod. Clay had to be satisfied with that for now.

Chapter 12

The first twisting streaks of falling snow thickened, very quickly becoming a screen of white that settled or lifted as the erratic wind, howling across the plateau, tore into it and then fell away again. Clay Reiner called a halt and, as Tug Morley pulled in on the reins, told Johnny, "You better get back inside. It's not going to be too comfortable up here, and I'm sure your mother would rather have you in with her."

He helped the boy climb down from the box, and then on a decision swung to the ground himself. He had a fresh mount, a bay from the stable at Trinidad, tied behind the coach. He got it off the towline, checked the cinch, brushed loose snow off the leather, and lifted himself into the saddle. His rifle, fully loaded, was in the scabbard; he had no reason to expect he would be needing it, though holdups weren't unknown in this rough country climbing toward Raton.

Actually he was thinking of the boulder in the roadway that had disabled the eastbound coach the night before last and held it up at Trinidad while repairs were made. In a storm like this one, with visibility shortened by the unceasing fall of snow, some such mishap was always possible. Better to be safe than to risk a needless accident to the coach and its precious cargo.

Reiner paused a moment for a word with his driver, then rode ahead as Morley yelled at his horses and the coach started forward. The snow was falling more heavily

with every minute. Reiner felt enclosed by it, shut off
from everything that lay beyond its shifting curtain and
from every muffled sound except the creak of leather and
the strike of his animal's hooves. The twisting road, hewn
by hand from hard lava rock, was really climbing now. It
entered a patch of timber, the trunks of the pines black
and ghostly and the rocky ground already showing white
as snow began to pile up. Reiner rode with his hat brim
pulled low against the chilly wetness, hunched in the
protection of his bulky poncho. He tried to ignore the
aching stiffness of his shoulder, injured in a war that
seemed ages ago in another world.

The road appeared to be open and clear of obstacles.
Not wanting to get too far ahead of the coach, he pulled
up to wait for it, moving the bay around to put their backs
to the snow-laden wind. The horse stomped restlessly as
Reiner listened to the wind wailing in the rocks and tearing at the heads of the dark-standing pines that crowded
close beside the roadway.

That wind nearly masked a sudden burst of gunshots.
Reiner stiffened, and the bay tossed its head as its
rider's hand involuntarily jerked on the reins. The wind,
blowing downslope and away, all but carried the shots out
of hearing. But there had been three of them, then a
squeal of horses and a sudden, horrifying crash. It was that
last which jarred Reiner free. Swearing, he gave the bay a
kick and sent it tearing back down the road, aware only
that some disaster had overtaken the coach and its
passengers.

From their slower rate of travel after Clay Reiner had
ridden away, Beth knew they must be climbing a grade,
with the stage teams fighting the pitch of this climb over
Raton Pass. Familiar with the route, she judged that Dick
Wootton's tollgate must not be far ahead, with the summit
of the pass a couple of miles beyond that. Afterward there
would be easier going, down the far slope of the Sangre de

Cristos. Santa Fe and the end of their journey still lay more than a day beyond, but they would know they were on the last leg.

Every person in the coach was willing for this to be over. Looking around at their silent faces in the gloom of the dreary day and with leather window shields lowered to keep out the weather, Beth felt her own weariness. She could only try to guess her mother's condition. Even young Johnny Winfield, who usually came down from the boot overflowing with excitement about the things he had seen and learned from Clay Reiner, was unusually silent this time. It was almost as though he had been given something that demanded long and sober thought.

Her own thoughts were troubled enough. She looked at the handsome features of the man seated opposite her, and asked herself what could be going on behind that frowning mask. She'd been so very sure of Frank Darby and of her own feelings. But now it seemed as if these months apart had worked some change in him—in both of them, perhaps. She still was baffled and troubled over his insistence that she marry him back there in Trinidad. And though she wasn't even sure why she had flatly refused, her rejection evidently had thrown him into a moody silence, and he had spoken hardly a word to her since. Yet this bothered her less, actually, than her unformed and nameless doubts. . . .

Above the familiar grind of wheels and the shuffling gait of the teams, she thought she heard a new and swelling sound, as though several horsemen were approaching up the road behind them and moving in a hurry. They had seen few travelers besides themselves. Out of curiosity, Beth pulled aside a corner of the leather window shield. She was surprised to note how fast the snow was falling and how much it already whitened the ground and clung to the dark branches of the pines. Through swirling flakes, she peered back along the stage road. At first she saw nothing. Then a quartet of horsemen loomed through the snowstorm, riding two and two.

Seeing the four of them together, Beth was reminded briefly of the similar number of deserters who were locked up back at the way station on Timpas Creek—unless they already were on their way under guard to Fort Lyon. But these men weren't soldiers; they were dressed in odds and ends of civilian clothing, bundled to the eyes against the storm and with slouch hats pulled low. When they sighted the stagecoach, she saw them rein in briefly, as though conferring. After that they came on again, quickly overtaking it. As they passed her, one gave Beth a piercing glance, but she could make out nothing of his features.

Then her heart almost stopped when she saw a gun slide into view from underneath his coat.

She might have cried out, but her voice failed her. They quickly passed beyond her range of vision, and she tried frantically to get around into a position to peer after them. At once she saw that all four were closing in on the forward end of the coach. Now a second gun appeared, and she heard a shout for the driver to halt. But Tug Morley had a different view of things. With a yell from his leathery lungs and a crack of the whip, he sent the stage horses leaping into their collars.

Cries of anger went up as the highwaymen saw the coach start to pull away from them. Handguns cracked flatly into the smother of falling snow. If they were shooting at the driver, he must have made a poor target hunched there on the seat while his horses settled into a scrambling run.

For a moment, Beth actually thought they were going to get away and leave the guns behind. But in the next instant there was an almost human scream of agony that told her one of the horses had been hit. Instinctively she grabbed the tug strap beside her window, squeezed her eyes shut, and braced herself. There was a violent jar as the horses collided with the fallen animal. She felt the coach slew around, careening wildly in loose snow, and heard her mother cry out in horror when all at once the stage began to tilt sideways on two of its great, iron-rimmed wheels.

As though in slow motion, the heavy coach seemed to climb ponderously, up and up, forever. Then it toppled.

To a grinding crash of timbers, it struck the rock-hewn roadway. Somehow Beth had kept her hold on the leather strap; her arm took a painful wrenching, but it saved her adding her own weight to the pileup of bodies as they were flung from their places. With her free hand she seized the edge of the window and hung there.

Suddenly everything was still. Her first clear thought was for her mother; she called out, but got no answer. Peering below her, she caught a glimpse of Harris McRae with both arms protectingly around Mary Hanlon. The Winfield woman and Johnny, though shaken up, seemed not to have been hurt.

Frank Darby freed himself from the tangle and staggered upright. He caught at Beth to steady her, and his face was white as he exclaimed, "Are you all right?"

Beth could only nod. She was staring at a slight trickle of blood across his forehead—he had lost his hat and must have taken a blow against some part of the coach framework. His expression was grim.

Darby turned his attention to the door that was just above his head as he stood, half bent in these cramped quarters. He reached up and fumbled with the latch, got it open, and flung back the heavy door, which slammed solidly against the side of the coach and knocked a streamer of loose snow in on top of them. When he thrust his head and upper body through the opening, Beth was surprised to see a gun in his hand—up until then she'd believed he was unarmed.

Less than a minute could have elapsed since the gunshot that dropped the team horse and caused the overturning of the stage. Beth had no idea what was happening outside, but apparently Darby thought he'd found a target. He fired and ducked back, and at once an answering bullet stamped into the framework of the coach above his head.

"Frank!" Beth cried in alarm. "You'll get yourself killed!"

He shook his head curtly, not looking at her, frowning as he listened. Somewhere near at hand, what sounded like a new gun had suddenly opened up. Darby, looking at Beth, silently mouthed the words: *the driver*. She nodded. Tug Morley had apparently been thrown clear when the coach went over, and now he was ready to give the attackers a fight. He fired twice, a third time. Somewhere a man cried out in startled pain.

The shooting died abruptly.

A strange stillness settled. Cautiously, Darby raised his head for another look through the door opening, and after a moment ducked back to announce, "I don't see anybody now."

"You mean they've gone?" Harris McRae demanded.

"Perhaps. Or maybe just pulled back into cover, in the trees, while they decide whether to go any further with this. The driver may be too good a shot for them. That yell I heard sounded to me as though he got one of them—I don't know how badly."

On his knees, leaning against one of the uptilted seats, McRae said angrily, "I want to know, where's that man Reiner? I thought it was his job to protect us! It's a wonder some of us weren't killed when this thing went over. And now, we sit and wait for them to come back and finish us off!"

"Not me!" Darby said quickly, as if reaching a sudden decision. "This is no good. If I'm to be killed, I want it in the open—not penned up where they can finish us off like shooting at fish in a barrel! I'm getting out of here."

He was already in motion. He reached up and laid his gun just outside the opening above his head, then caught the sides of the door frame with both hands and hauled himself through with greater agility than Beth would have expected. He instantly flattened himself—but no bullet greeted him. Thrusting his head into the opening, he said, "All right so far. Beth—give me your hands."

She shook her head. "I'd better stay—"

"No! I want you with *me*. Whatever happens." And before she knew what was happening, he had seized her by the arms and, with surprising strength, lifted her up beside him. "Quick!" he ordered. "Over the side!" And giving her no time to protest, he swung her across the edge of what had been the roof. She caught at the baggage rail to help lower herself to the ground, and an instant later he leaped down beside her. His gun was again in his hand.

Beth protested, "But I should be with Mother!"

He dismissed that with a shake of the head. "She's doing fine. After all, she's got your uncle to look after her," he pointed out with more than a hint of sarcasm.

Beth looked around her through the falling snow. She could see now it was one of the lead team that had taken the bullet—it lay stiffening while the remaining animals stood uneasy in the harness, upset and trying to move around as they pawed at the ground. She caught a glimpse of Tug Morley crouched behind a boulder; he waggled his gun barrel when she caught his eye. After that, keeping behind the protection of the coach, she joined Frank Darby in his search for the enemy.

Things seemed unnaturally silent. An upturned wheel of the coach was still lazily spinning. Across the roadway, the shifting snow was like a curtain between them and the scattered stand of timber. She asked in a hushed voice, "You really think they're over there? Then why don't they do something? What can they be waiting for?"

"Who knows," he said with a shrug. "Perhaps they're just cautious. They've already been bloodied, and they can't know for certain how many guns we actually have.

Perhaps they'll decide to give the whole thing up as a bad job. . . ."

Suddenly his head whipped around, and she saw what had caught his attention. A horseman had just rounded into view on the road above them. He came at a good clip, a dark figure in a shapeless poncho. Beth turned to speak— and her breath caught as she saw the revolver rising in Darby's hand. "Frank!" she protested. "No!" Frantically she grabbed at his arm, trying to pull the gun aside. "Don't! *Don't!* It's Clay!"

He gave no sign of hearing. He was intent on his purpose—it showed in the look of his face, so fiercely set that for a moment she scarcely recognized him. Above them the horseman had pulled in, making himself almost a stationary target. Next instant, Beth's protest was lost in the roar of the gun.

The jar of it in Darby's hand shuddered through his wrist to her clutching fingers. Horrified, she saw the rider give a jerk that said he might be hit, or perhaps only startled by a near and unexpected bullet. Darby, for one, seemed to think he had missed; suddenly she realized he meant to try again. With ears still ringing she cried, almost sobbing now, "Frank! I tell you—that's *Clay Reiner!*"

He turned his head to look at her. The expression of ferocity that had alarmed her slowly altered, and then he peered again at the horseman who was sitting motionless staring in the direction of the coach. He said, "Oh, my God! I think you're right! It *is* Reiner. I might have killed him!"

With a shake of the head, he lowered the gun. But Beth found herself haunted by the thing she had read in his face, and by a fleeting thought, instantly dismissed: He might have known all along who the rider was, and only her presence had kept him from deliberately shooting Clay out of the saddle!

* * *

The shock of horror Clay Reiner felt at his first sight
of the wrecked stagecoach was enough to make his hand
jerk convulsively on the reins, bringing his mount to a
stop. For a frozen instant of time he sat peering into the
whipping snow screen, fighting a constriction in his chest.
The dead lead horse, with the other animals tangled and
struggling in the harness, told clearly enough what had
happened. He saw no other movement at all, nor any sign
of attackers. The sporadic burst of gunfire had ceased; an
eerie stillness lay over the scene before him.

The shot, when it came, seemed to Clay to have been
fired from near the coach, though this storm blotted up
sounds and confused directions—so he could be mistaken.
But there was no mistaking the sound of the bullet that
splatted against a rock face so near as to make him flinch.
That had been aimed at him; even his startled horse knew
it! He settled the animal and brought up his own pistol,
but he had no target—not even a wisp of powder smoke,
which the ground wind would have quickly scattered.

Then a figure waved to him from behind a boulder,
not far from the coach, and he recognized Tug Morley, the
driver. Morley was signaling, pointing across the road
toward the thin scatter of pine that was ahead and to
Reiner's left. Almost as if to confirm what the driver was
trying to tell him, two guns opened up simultaneously
among the black tree trunks. Reiner even saw a brief spurt
of muzzle flame. Morley dropped behind the boulder, but
then his answering shot indicated he wasn't hit.

Reiner was already in motion. A yank at his reins sent
the bay scrambling out of the road and into rocks and
timber. He dismounted and stood a moment peering around
him and listening. Hastily then, he made a quick tie of the
reins to a low-hanging pine branch. He slid his rifle from
the saddle boot and started working his way cautiously
forward.

It seemed strangely quiet, with only the moaning
wind causing branches to creak overhead. Sporadically

there came the sound of a shot somewhere ahead of him, which was answered by Tug Morley over near the downed stagecoach. Reiner found himself thinking, *I hope he's got a good supply of bullets and caps!* The strategy was somewhat puzzling. Having wrecked the coach, one might have expected the attackers to rush in to finish the job—grab off the mail sack or whatever it was they thought they wanted—while those on board were still too shaken to fight them off. As it was, Reiner couldn't see that they were getting anywhere.

A moment later, he thought perhaps he understood.

Somebody was coming. He stiffened as he heard the man's approach, heard him breathing and muttering a curse as his boot slipped on loose snow. Reiner tightened his grip on the rifle as he waited. Suddenly the man was in sight, looming through the white smother. He had his head down, a slouch hat concealing his face, a gun swinging at the end of his arm as he concentrated on maneuvering through the treacherous footing. Reiner couldn't imagine why he should seem oddly familiar, but his purpose at least was suddenly clear: While the rest held Tug Morley pinned down with sporadic firing, his job was to circle across the road and behind the boulder, to take the driver unprepared.

If the man didn't look up, he would pass within a yard of the place where Reiner stood. Grimly, Reiner waited and let him come on. Then he shouted, "That's far enough. *Freeze!*"

The man did, for one split second, and then made a frantic effort to turn. But surprise and haste rendered him clumsy, and Reiner could have shot him easily if he wanted. Instead, he took a stride and brought the rifle's stock around, solidly, against the fellow's head.

Even cushioned by the hat, it was enough to drop him without a sound. He went down in a heap, losing both hat and pistol. And when Reiner rolled him face up in the snow, he gasped in pure astonishment—for he recognized one of the army deserters he himself had locked up in a tack shed at the way station on Timpas Creek.

In that moment he could only stare, not understanding. Then he felt a slow chill of dread as he realized what this might imply as to the fates of Milt Gentry, his wife, and their stock handler. He had to put that thought out of his mind for the present. At least he knew now who had attacked the stage—and, probably, what they wanted. Trooper Lake had struck him as a man who wouldn't give up a notion easily, and he surely had the strength of will to keep the rest in line. . . .

The one he had felled wouldn't be going anywhere soon, so it was safe to leave him for the time being. Reiner lifted the unconscious man's revolver and tucked it behind his waistband. Then, with his rifle ready, he started ahead through the scatter of trees.

The wind whipped up in a sudden, crazy fury that seemed to blow from half a dozen directions at once, filling his eyes with snow and blinding him, while the roar in his ears blanked out all other sound. Each step he took was a peril, since he couldn't be sure what lay just ahead. Snow-slick rock tried to cost him his footing; brush dragged at his clothing. He bore to his left, thinking that this ought to put his enemies somewhere between him and the stage road. If he were lucky, he might come in from the rear as they had hoped to do to Tug Morley.

Very near at hand, a couple of gunshots warned him the enemy was close. And as he halted, moving behind the scant protection of the trunk of a jack pine, a shift in the wind lifted the white curtain, allowing him a frozen glimpse of the scene before him. There could be no mistaking the shape of big Trooper Lake, spread-legged as he peered in the direction of the road. A little beyond, another man sat slumped with his back against a tree, evidently in pain. A third man bent over him as though trying to help. They had managed to rid themselves of the telltale army uniforms, but these were what was left of the deserters.

Suddenly Lake made a convulsive movement that indicated he had sighted something in the road below. Reiner looked and saw it: A man had materialized there, to halt and stand staring at whatever he had found on the ground in front of him. There was only enough time to make out that the man was Harris McRae and that he seemed unmindful of the peril he was in. Already Lake was raising his revolver. With only seconds in which to act, Clay Reiner shouted, "McRae! *Drop!*"

Lake's shot, and his target's fall, came so near together that it was impossible to say whether or not McRae had been hit. Reiner was given no time to wonder about it; Trooper Lake had heard the warning shout, and now he was turning to find the source of it. Across a narrow distance, he and Reiner stared at each other. And the big man fired.

A bullet clipped pine bark within inches of Reiner. Mouth set hard, Clay stepped into the open with his rifle butt pressed against his hip. He threw a shot that made the deserter fall back a step. Lake tried a second time, but the hurried bullet went wide. And Clay Reiner stood his ground, worked the lever, and shot again. To the boom of the rifle, he saw Trooper Lake get flung backward, striking a tree trunk and dropping face downward. The loose way he fell was enough to show he was dead.

Reiner shook himself and remembered to look for the remaining pair of deserters. The man seated on the ground remained there, motionless, chin sunk forward on his chest. But the other one had vanished. Reiner ran forward, passing the body of Lake without a glance. As he had suspected, the man seated against the tree had at some point in the fight taken a bullet in the upper part of his body. Reiner saw blood, and a crude attempt someone had made at a bandage. A pistol lay beside him, and

Reiner halted long enough to pick it up and toss it beyond reach.

At the same moment, he became aware of hoofbeats as somewhere to the north of him a horse broke into a run, going away. The sound was almost instantly swallowed and muffled by the snow that blanketed this approach to Raton Pass. Reiner lowered his rifle, realizing the last remaining deserter had already made good his escape. Well—there was no chance of stopping him now. Clay would have to be satisfied with three out of four, including the one who had been their ringleader.

But for the moment the prisoners would have to wait. Reiner's concern, just now, was for the people in the wrecked stagecoach. He turned and hurried down to the place where Harris McRae stood motionless, as though oblivious to everything except what lay at his feet. And now, as Reiner made out the figure lying with face turned up into the falling snow, a kind of sickness knotted swiftly inside him.

A shape that slight and small could belong to only one person. It was with a cry of angry protest that he looked upon the still face of Johnny Winfield.

Chapter 13

Harris McRae looked like a man in shock. Clay Reiner handed him his rifle to hold, then kneeled down on one knee, fearful of what he was going to discover. Johnny's eyes were closed. He had lost his hat, and at once Reiner saw the ugly stain of blood in his hair and in the snow beneath his head. His own fingers shook with dread, and he was reluctant to examine the extent of the damage.

He scarcely heard the explanation that came spilling out of McRae, in words that tumbled over one another: "Reiner, I just don't know what could have got into the boy! We were all shaken up, but no one really hurt, when the stage went over. My niece and young Darby climbed out, but the rest felt safer staying where we were. There were guns going off. I tried to keep the others posted, as much as I could make out, on what was happening. Suddenly, before anyone knew what he was up to, Johnny here went clambering out of the coach, and his mother cried out that he'd taken the gun from her reticule. I don't know what he thought he was going to do with it, but—well, *somebody* had to go after him!" He added hoarsely, "I was just too late!"

Reiner had opened the boy's jacket and had an ear against his chest. He waved McRae to silence. A moment later he said, "Maybe not quite."

"What! D'you mean—?"

Not answering, Reiner felt for the large arteries of Johnny's throat, scowling in concentration. Suddenly he exclaimed, "Yes! There's a pulse—a strong, steady one. This may only be a scalp wound, after all!"

"Oh, let's hope to God you're right!" McRae stammered. "He's a good lad. And that Amelia Winfield is the best! It just wouldn't be fair for anything to happen—now—after what both have been through." He added quickly, as though other things had driven the question out of his head, "But what about the trouble here? Is it all over?"

Reiner nodded. "One man got away, one is dead, a couple more out of action. It was that same bunch of deserters—I guess they had an idea, and they wouldn't let go of it."

"But—the people at the station where we left them—?"

"I'm worried about them," Clay admitted. "But right now this youngster is our concern. I hate to try and move him, but there's no choice." Gently he eased the limp shape of Johnny Winfield into his arms and got to his feet. "There's his hat and the gun he took. Bring them."

"Reiner. Wait. . . ."

The man's urgency made him pause, still holding his limp burden.

"Something I have to say to you." Harris McRae looked suddenly flushed; the words seemed forced from him. "I'm not so big a fool," he said, "that I don't realize you saved my life just now. Perhaps I don't understand why you'd bother. I haven't made things any smoother for you since we started this trip."

Reiner met his look coldly. "It's not worth talking about."

"Just the same," the other man went on doggedly, "I'm going to say this, and you're going to listen! Reiner, I'm a man who's worked and fought for what he has, and I'm proud of it. Perhaps a little too proud. Too proud not to resent taking orders, or criticism, from somebody I judge hasn't done as well! Beth keeps telling me that I've been wrong about you—that you're one of Tom Hanlon's best men. It's clear to me now that she probably knows what she's talking about."

He had come as near to an apology, it seemed, as this stiff-necked man was capable of doing. It did little to ease Reiner's dislike of Harris McRae. Still, if he had unbent this far, he deserved something in return. "All right," Clay Reiner said curtly. "We'll call it a truce. I suppose I'm ready for one if you are. But we can't afford to stand here any longer talking about it. Come along."

An answering nod from McRae, and they turned again toward the coach with the hurt boy, while the wind whipped stinging swirls of snow around them in suddenly increased fury.

They were met by the driver, Tug Morley, and by Mary Hanlon and Amelia Winfield. Johnny's mother uttered a low moan when she saw Reiner's burden. He spoke quickly in an attempt to reassure her. "Don't upset yourself. I really doubt it's as bad as it looks. You've got a brave youngster, Mrs. Winfield," he added. "You, and your husband, too, have every reason to be proud!"

Having laid the hurt boy gently in the lee of the overturned coach, he then turned to Harris McRae with an order to collect blankets and anything else available to make Johnny as warm and comfortable as possible. Also, there was a tarpaulin in the boot, under the driver's seat, that could be fixed up to make a temporary windbreak. As McRae hurried off to see about this, Reiner used as few words as possible to answer the worried questions he was getting from the others.

He had been searching anxiously for Beth Hanlon; he saw her now and was tremendously relieved that she seemed to have come through unhurt. But there was no chance to speak to her, because Tug Morley demanded attention, wanting to know what they should do next. Three of the horses seemed to be all right, but damage to the stagecoach would be hard to judge until it was lifted back up on its wheels.

Reiner led the driver across the road to the place where he had left his horse tied. "Take him," he ordered. "Get up to Wootton's and fetch us some more men—a block and tackle—whatever you think is needed. Bring a wagon while you're at it. We have a couple of prisoners to haul, as well as the passengers and freight. You know the situation. I don't have to warn you about losing any time."

"Right, boss." Morley rose to the saddle and at once was on his way up the road to the pass; the storm quickly swallowed him.

Reiner approached his prisoners. The one he had felled with a blow of his rifle stock was conscious but dazed. He groaned and cursed when Reiner dragged him to his feet and forced the man to march ahead of him through the trees. They found Trooper Lake already stiffening, his body mounding over under a pileup of drifting snow. The wounded man was still alive, huddled under the tree where his friends had placed him. Reiner left him there for the moment while he demanded to be shown where the horses were tied, but he wasn't too surprised when he discovered nothing more than the plowed-up snow, marked by their hooves. He had assumed the last of the deserters would have set the rest of the animals loose as he was escaping, in an effort to hold up pursuit.

The wounded prisoner had taken a bullet through the upper part of his chest; it was a question of just how bad a wound it was and what his chances were of surviving it. There was little enough they could do for him, except to get him up and half lead, half carry him down to the coach. Reiner settled him there under the improvised windbreak, where his passengers huddled wrapped in blankets and tried to keep warm while they waited for rescue to arrive. Harris McRae volunteered to keep an eye on both prisoners, for which purpose Reiner issued him one of the captured weapons.

And then Beth was beside him, and he knew something was wrong even before she said, "Clay! I don't know what's become of Frank. . . ."

"What!"

Somehow, in all that had been going on, he hadn't missed Frank Darby. Now as he looked around, immediately aware the man was nowhere in sight, Beth went on to explain, "He was right beside me—and then, suddenly, he wasn't. I have no idea where he might have gone to. I tried looking, but in this storm I was afraid of being turned around and getting lost myself. And—well, Frank simply isn't at home in this sort of country, not the way *we* are. I'm worried about him!"

As she had a right to be, Reiner thought. "You should have told me sooner!"

"This was the first chance I've had."

"All right." He placed a reassuring hand on her arm. "I don't imagine anything's happened; still, I'll have a look around. Tell me where you last saw him."

For all his personal dislike of the man, Reiner had no reason to think of Frank Darby as any sort of a coward who would run from a gunfight. Trying to guess at what had happened, he thought it much more likely Darby would have had some idea of taking the fight to the enemy, but in an indirect route to avoid walking straight into their guns. If that were the case, Darby, not being an outdoorsman, might possibly have been confused by the fury of the storm and lost his sense of direction.

Reiner tried to pick up signs of the man, but by now the snow cover around the coach had been hopelessly trampled. It was almost by chance that he discovered a line of footprints that were almost certainly Darby's, and set out at once to follow them through a broken terrain of boulders and scrub growth. His luck failed to hold. In a very few minutes, his search brought him out into the open where, in the sweep of the wind across loose snow, any trace of prints was instantly erased.

Reiner halted. He could see nothing moving anywhere

in the whiteness of the storm that enclosed and isolated him. He turned in a slow half circle, searching. He cupped his hands to his mouth and called Frank Darby's name, waited, and called again. His voice seemed muffled and torn to shreds almost as it left his lips. And though he strained to catch any answering cry, he could hear nothing at all above the whine of the wind.

Slowly he lowered his hands and shook his head. There was nothing more for him to do alone. With men from Wootton's, and lanterns against the premature fall of night, he would be able to mount a full-scale search. But with dusk close at hand and the thermometer already beginning to fall, Reiner began to feel the weight of doubt. It was altogether possible they would never find any trace of Frank Darby here in this country under the shoulder of Raton Mountain.

Clay Reiner felt a cold knot begin to form inside him at the prospect of having to return empty-handed and report the situation to Beth.

Beth Hanlon, leaving the bedroom where her mother and Amelia Winfield held vigil over Johnny, approached the public room of Wootton's tollhouse with a mixture of hope and dread as she heard a rumbling of voices and realized who was speaking. In the doorway she halted, looking in on the low-ceilinged room with its blazing fireplace, its native furnishings, and the walls that held Wootton's trophies—mounted heads of deer and bear, racks of antlers and firearms.

Richens Wootton, better known as Uncle Dick Wootton—fur trader, Indian fighter, friend of Kit Carson, and himself a legendary figure in the opening of the West—stood with his back to the fire, talking to Clay Reiner and Harris McRae. The latter two had apparently just entered and had brought the cold of the night clinging to their clothing. Beth's uncle still carried a lighted lantern, which he now proceeded to blow out and place on the floor next to the outside entrance. Reiner was speaking as both men stripped out of their winter gear. Beth caught the name of Frank Darby, and the very look of the men was enough to tell her there was no good news.

Dick Wootton was a solid figure of a man in his early fifties, rough hewn as this Colorado Territory, with graying hair that fell to his shoulders. He shook his head now as he told Clay, "I'd say you done all you could. There's certainly no call to blame yourself."

But Reiner burst out, "Dammit, he's out there somewhere! We should have found him!"

"I'm not so sure. Remember—I knew him, too. I pegged him for a man who wasn't going to let anyone tell him anything. And in this country, a city fellow with that kind of attitude can be his own worst enemy. He'll do himself in, and there's nothing anybody can do to prevent it."

Harris McRae put in a word of reassurance. "The man's right, you know," he told Reiner. "Look at *me*—I could have gotten lost in that storm myself, just while we were looking for him. But I was lucky enough to be with someone who knew what he was doing!"

Reiner didn't appear to be listening. He had caught sight of Beth, and his face was pale as he came over to her. He took a deep breath, as though steeling himself to speak. "I guess you heard," he said bluntly. "We failed, Beth. There were two others with us, and we combed all that area; but not a trace! Please try to believe that we only quit when we saw it was hopeless."

"It's the truth, girl," her uncle said. In contrast to his previous hostility, in the past few hours Harris McRae had become Clay Reiner's champion. "It was a thorough search. I still don't see how we could have missed finding him. But there it is. I just don't want you blaming Reiner."

Wootton put in quickly, "He ain't the one to give up when there's any hope left."

"Of course." Beth spoke from conviction. At the moment she was more troubled by her own confusing reactions. There was horror and distress at the possible fate of anyone lost out there, with the temperature plummeting as night deepened. But aside from that, there was somehow less of a sense of personal tragedy than she would have expected. Something odd had happened to her relationship with the man she was engaged to marry—she could not understand exactly what, or how.

She felt Clay's hand on her shoulder, heard his exclamation: "Beth—are you all right?"

"Yes—yes," she stammered, breaking through the contradictory mood that had descended upon her. From his frown, she knew Reiner was not at all reassured, but there was no way she could have hoped to explain.

As though from a distance, her uncle's voice reached her, asking a question she knew concerned him very much. "What about Johnny Winfield?"

"The boy?" Dick Wootton answered him. "He's not too bad hurt—by a fraction of an inch! The bullet grazed him bad enough to knock him out, probably gave him a concussion. But the women got him patched up, and in my judgment he'll soon be as good as new."

Harris McRae said earnestly, "Thank God. I've grown quite fond of that youngster."

Beth had her own emotions under control. "Would you like to see him?"

"We certainly would," Clay Reiner said.

She led them down the hall to the little room where Johnny had been placed after being brought up by wagon from the scene of the wreck. It was small, with scarcely space for more than the bed in which the boy lay, his eyes closed and his face almost as white as the bandage around his head. His mother and Mary Hanlon were both there. Reiner forestalled their questions with a quick shake of the head, saying, "I'm afraid we didn't find anything. We've come to see about the boy. He looks to be asleep."

But Johnny's eyes had opened at the sound of Reiner's voice. Beth saw the way they lit up, how he even attempted a grin for this man he had come to admire so much. She saw, too, how Clay's own weathered features softened, losing some of the strain that the responsibilities of a disaster-haunted stagecoach journey had put there.

While the others watched, Clay stepped over to the bed. "How you feeling, partner?"

"No better'n I should, I guess," Johnny said, looking up at him, the grin fading a little. "After what I did, you gonna bawl me out?"

"Would you say you've got it coming?" Clay countered, sternly. "What on earth did you suppose you were up to?"

Johnny swallowed. "Being a hero, I reckon. Somebody yelled that you was going after them deserters, all by yourself. Looked to me like you could use some help!" He added, a little ruefully, "I guess you could say it was like what you told me—about seeing a job that needed doing. Only, I guess I near got myself killed trying to do it. Mr. McRae, too." He shook his head a little on the pillow, and his mouth began to tremble. "I'm sorry. I really am!"

"You also know you caused your mother a lot of anxiety?" Reiner waited for the boy's nod of admission. But then, with that point made, Clay smiled, and Beth noted his change of tone. "Well, don't be too hard on yourself. Personally, I'll always remember you came to help me. That took real courage. All you have to do after this is learn to use better judgment as to the size of the jobs you tackle!"

The boy's grin returned. "I'll try," Johnny said.

Clay touched him on the shoulder, accepting that for a promise. "Good enough. Right now your job is to stay where you are and get well enough to travel—maybe by the next stage that comes through."

Alarm almost lifted the youngster off his pillow. "You— you wouldn't go on without me?"

"It's best that way," his mother put in quickly. "Until we're sure you're better."

153

"But I'm better *now*! I'm doing fine! We've come so close to the end now, and—" He appealed to Clay. "I want to see my pa!"

To Beth, watching from the foot of the bed, it seemed that an urgent and unspoken message passed between the man and the boy. After the briefest hesitation, Clay Reiner nodded. "All right, Johnny. Don't fret about it. The main thing you need is rest. We'll talk it over in the morning, see how you feel then and what your mother thinks. Okay, partner?"

Johnny smiled in agreement and settled back obediently to close his eyes.

Later, Dick Wootton got Reiner aside to compare notes. "If you're wondering about your prisoners, the ones that are alive should both make it. I've got them locked up—safe, this time! I threatened to work them over some, trying to get them to tell me how they busted loose from that station at Timpas Creek. Before I hardly got started, it was a contest to see which of them could talk the loudest and fastest!"

"And what do they say?" Reiner demanded quickly. "How about the people at the station?"

"All done for! The stationmaster and his wife, and a stock handler. Naturally," he went on, as the other absorbed the shock of this, "they put all the killings on the dead one, the fellow they call Lake."

"Naturally!" Reiner said bleakly. "Though I'm inclined to think it's probably true. It sounds like him."

"They say he tricked your man Gentry, got his gun away from him, and shot everything that moved. They took clothes and grub and horses from the corral, and rode bareback until they were able to swipe more animals and saddle gear at Trinidad. Did they really have some crazy idea about collecting ransom from your boss?"

Reiner nodded. "Once they got the notion in their heads, I guess nothing but bullets could knock it out!" He added, "Can you hold them here for the military?"

"No problem," Wootton assured him. "Meanwhile, if this storm quits, by daylight I figure to take a look myself and see if I can turn up any kind of clue as to what happened to your man Darby. He could be out there wandering in circles, freezing to death. Or he could have fallen down a hole and broke his neck. I'm afraid there's a good chance you may never find out."

"I'm afraid you're right!"

Behind the bleak admission lay a nagging doubt: *Was it my fault? Will Beth come to think that it was?* But it was a useless treadmill to find himself trapped on; Reiner shrugged the thought away and went on to other matters.

"I've got to make some arrangement for the Timpas Creek station. Gentry had another stock handler, a fellow named Bert Collins, who went to Fort Lyon with word of the deserters. Collins ought to be back by now. He's a good man—he should be able to take charge and keep things operating. But I'd like to send down one of the boys from here to help out. Later, Tom Hanlon will have to decide on a permanent replacement for Milt Gentry. What about tonight?" he asked. "Can you put my passengers up for me?"

"No problem," Wootton replied.

In the big barn, which was part of the complex of buildings making up Wootton's station, Reiner found his men completing their inspection of the coach they had hauled up from the site of the accident. It loomed toward the rafters, a scarred and battered veteran of the trails, lantern glow revealing its graceful lines and solid construction.

After his years devoted to the Hanlon Stage Line, Reiner still kept a deep pride and respect for the big Concords—they were built to last, to give unfailing service, and to withstand the worst of mishaps. The careful craftsmanship and design Abbot and Downing had put into their sturdy red vehicles had carried the name of their firm, and of their New Hampshire city, to the remotest reaches of the continent.

"We been over her from stem to stern," Tug Morley assured him. "Can't find any real damage, barring a few more gouges in her paint job—as if that was anything new. Give us five minutes to put a team into the harness, and we're ready to take off again."

"Fine," Reiner said. "But not now. I've decided to wait till morning."

The driver stared at him. "You mean it? What about the schedule?"

"Far as this run's concerned, the schedule is already shot to pieces. Nothing much we can do about it. By morning, this storm should have blown itself out. If not, I'd rather face it by daylight. And then, there's our passengers. They've been through enough, and they deserve a decent night's rest. By that time, the boy may be in good enough shape, and he and his mother will be able to go on with us. So, get some sleep yourself. I hope to take off early."

Reiner had a word with one of the other company men, Jeff Roerig, about the situation at the way station on Timpas Creek. "Bert Collins is alone now. Come daylight, I want you to saddle up and get down there with a message for him. Tell Bert he's in charge, and the two of you are responsible for keeping the station running and the stages going through. When I've seen Tom Hanlon, we'll be making some kind of permanent arrangement."

Afterward, leaving the barn, Reiner stood a moment in the doorway with lantern light streaming past him into the compound, picking up the streaks and swirls of snow. Except where the wind swept it into glittering clouds, the snow didn't seem as thick now as it had been. Clay was able to make out the sprawl of Wootton's adobe roadhouse, its window, showing yellow squares of lamplight. He could even glimpse the single black pole of the tollgate, barring the road—no traveller, he thought, was apt to be abroad to use the road tonight.

This place was still a couple of miles below the summit of Raton Pass. Tomorrow, once they had crossed the pass and started down the spine of the Sangre de Cristos, the weather should begin to improve. If they were lucky, perhaps the rest of this journey would turn out to be uneventful.

He would keep his fingers crossed.

Frank Darby, watching from a screen of brush one hundred yards from the station building, instantly spotted Clay Reiner as he stood silhouetted against the barn doorway. Nothing could prevent him from recognizing a man he had come to hate this intensely. The pistol lifted in his hand, almost of its own volition, but then reason lowered it again. A handgun shot at night, under such conditions, was useless. More than that, even if he should manage to bring the bastard down, the sound of the gun would betray him and ruin everything. And Darby didn't think of himself as one to be easily swayed by fatal impulses.

A moment later the barn door swung to, shutting away the light and removing any temptation. He put up the gun and stood waiting, giving no heed to the bone-chilling night and the wet wind against his face—he was a man who gave no quarter to mere physical discomfort when his personal aims were at stake.

He picked up Reiner again, crossing a lighted window and then vanishing as a door of the main station building briefly opened and closed. The night settled around him; Darby began to have a feeling that he and the horse tied near him in the brush were the only living things abroad in it. Building lights began to darken, and still he continued to wait. His only concession to the growing cold, as the night grew older, was to tramp back and forth beating his arms against his body to keep the circulation stirring.

Finally, after an undetermined length of time, Darby decided the time was right to make his move.

He turned to his horse, swept the saddle clear of snow, and mounted. It was one of the deserters' animals.

Capturing it in the confused aftermath of the gun battle had suggested a daring scheme that should solve all his problems for him. He'd found it simple enough avoiding the searchers he had heard calling for him. It left him now with one final hurdle confronting him, and his nerves were strung tight as he approached it.

The snow underfoot muffled his animal's hooves as they came in toward the station at a careful walk. Ground wind, he knew, soon would smooth out the tracks and leave no trace of him. Nothing moved around the buildings; an occasional spark from a chimney spilled out and was swept streaming away. Darby rode directly toward the barrier of the tollgate, reasoning that no one would be expecting to see a horseman on the road at such an hour of such a night. He looked cautiously around, checking and listening for danger.

It was the work of a moment, leaning from his saddle, to lift the gate, duck beneath it, and let the bar drop again behind him. Darby actually smiled a little in relief at the ease with which everything was working out so far. He didn't dally. He gave the horse a kick and sent it on along the road toward the head of the pass up ahead. Wootton's station was quickly swallowed in the storm and left behind.

Chapter 14

Clay Reiner had meant what he said about forgetting the stage schedule. They had fallen so many hours behind that catching up now was out of the question. Meanwhile, his passengers had been through enough; there would be no sense in punishing them needlessly. So it was full daylight when he ordered the coach readied and brought to the door of the station.

Johnny Winfield looked a good deal better this morning, though still weak from the blood he'd lost. But he was game and anxious to finish this last leg of the journey that had brought him and his mother almost across a continent. Reiner didn't have the heart to refuse him. They got him up and warmly dressed, and when everything else was ready, the boy was placed in his seat in the stage and made comfortable there.

The team horses stomped and blew streamers of breath into the still morning air. The snow had stopped, the wind had fallen off, and a thick and chill fog held among the rocks and scrub timber. Clay mounted his horse, scouting the fog-shrouded road ahead of the coach. The tollgate was raised, and Tug Morley yelled his animals into motion.

Dick Wootton wasn't there to see them off. At first dawn, he had set out with another man to make a daylight search for Frank Darby. The fact that they hadn't yet returned told Reiner of their lack of success—and if anyone knew this stretch of rugged country, it would have to be Dick Wootton. But what on earth could have happened to Darby, unless he'd stumbled into a pitfall or perhaps crawled into some natural shelter? If he was dead, would they ever find his body? And how long before Beth recovered from the shock of it? Such questions were like an indissoluble lump of lead that settled inside him and stayed there as he led the stagecoach through drifting layers of fog up to the summit of Raton Pass.

Wind had combed the surface of the road, in places even sweeping it clean of snow. There would have been little to show if anyone else had been up here ahead of them in the past several hours. But now the road dropped swiftly through the gorge called the Devil's Gate, where the reckless breed of men who drove the stages liked to let their teams out for a slapdash descent to lower country beyond. Reiner, however, had given Tug Morley strict orders to ride his brake and hold his animals to a steady pace, running no risk of further accidents.

It began to look as if fate had dealt them a new hand with the crossing of the plateau. Almost at once, the weather improved. They dropped down out of the fogbank that turned the world gray and colorless, the cloud ceiling thinned and became faintly tinged with blue, and the sun burst forth. It was a pale winter sun without much warmth, but enough to burn away the mist and to flood the steaming land, and its far-off vista of mesas and lowlands, with a welcome brightness that couldn't fail to raise the most discouraged traveler's spirits.

The change of scenery was equally dramatic. Within a few miles they had dropped almost a thousand feet, nearly out of the zone of yesterday's storm. The snow cover became thinner and sparser, finally becoming a patchy scurf along treetops and hollows and the shadowed sides of boulders.

At each stop, Reiner checked on the improving condition of Johnny Winfield. The boy's eyes were brighter, his color good, his enthusiasm higher as the long journey drew to a close. Reiner asked Amelia, "Did your husband know when he should expect you?"

"Only in a general way, I suppose," she told him. "The last chance I had to write was at St. Louis. I told him what train we'd be taking and when we were scheduled to connect with the stage line at Hays City."

"He probably could have figured from that. But we're almost exactly a day late. I hope he hasn't been worrying. . . ."

The day passed without incident—in itself a welcome change for both Reiner and his passengers. A late meal stop was made at Maxwell's Ranch on the Cimarron, a place with a big house and a Pennsylvania-style barn and a new flour mill. As they loaded again afterward, Reiner told the boy, "Not too much farther now. You'll eat breakfast at Fort Union."

He had told Johnny something about that installation, one of the largest and most important in the Southwest. Its storehouse and arsenal had been a prize in the early days of the Civil War, and he'd told the boy about the battle at Glorieta Pass, in 1862, when the defeat of Texas soldiers had kept the Confederacy from laying its hands on the army's supplies and ammunition, and helped hold New Mexico Territory for the Union.

As they came in on Fort Union in the small hours of the night, anyone would surely have been impressed with the sheer size of the place, with its parade ground and the many adobe buildings that surrounded it. It conveyed a sense of military power even now, asleep under the stars and a high-riding full moon that paled the scattered splash of lamplight. A sentry presented his rifle in salute as the coach rolled in, finally halting in front of the barn and stage station that Tom Hanlon maintained on the site.

The local agent, a man named Sanford, came stumbling out of his sleeping quarters, swollen-eyed and grumbling and carrying a lantern. "Where the hell you people been?" he yelled up at the men on the box. "You lost your calendar? Don't you know this is Monday already? You were supposed to have got here this time yesterday!"

Reiner left it for the driver to explain. The stock handler had appeared, yawning and pulling on his clothes, to begin the routine of changing teams. Reiner climbed down and went to open the door and lower the iron step for Amelia Winfield, saying, "This is it, ma'am. You're here at last. . . ."

He helped her out, and only then did they see the tall man in an officer's uniform who stood waiting for her. With a cry of greeting, Amelia rushed into his arms, while Reiner hurriedly busied himself with extricating her luggage from the rear boot.

He heard the soldier say, "I couldn't help but worry a little when the time came and passed and you didn't arrive. Still, I knew there could be any number of reasons, and I've got faith in the men who run this stage line. And tonight I had the strongest hunch I'd finally be seeing you. . . ."

Now Amelia introduced him to Clay Reiner, who was impressed with this man who had been a hero of the Union during the recent war. Lieutenant John Winfield, he decided, was a man who would inspire respect and confidence; his grip was strong, his bearing erect, his glance direct and level. There was a strong hint of what young Johnny would look like when his features had firmed into manhood.

Suddenly the man's head lifted sharply and he gasped, "My God!" Johnny was just now getting down from the coach, his movements uncertain, his hat set askew by the bandage around his head. His father exclaimed hoarsely, "What's happened? What in the world is wrong with him?"

"If you ask my opinion," Clay said, "there's not a lot wrong with *this* youngster, Winfield! You've got a son to be proud of—the makings of a hero, like his pa!" And as Amelia gave the boy a steadying hand down to the ground, Reiner offered a terse account of their troubles with the deserters and the battle at Raton Pass. "There was some shooting. Johnny plunged in to help and got in the way of a bullet. But it looks a lot worse than it really is," he said. "Have the post surgeon take a look at him. I think he'll tell you the same."

There was a silence as he finished. Father and son faced each other, and Reiner sensed the awkward constraint between them. It was Winfield who found his voice to ask, a little stiffly, "What about it, son? How are you feeling?"

In the same manner, Johnny replied, "I'm fine, Pa." But then the dam broke in a rush of enthusiasm: "And we had the swellest trip! Plenty of excitement! And all thanks to Mr. Reiner—he got us through everything!"

To which his mother added, "It's the way he says, John. We owe Mr. Reiner a lot."

John Winfield turned to give the other man a long and probing look. He nodded. "You have my thanks," he said soberly. "I hope we get to be better acquainted."

"I do, too."

With an exclamation, Winfield turned again to his wife and son. "I almost forgot! These came through only yesterday!"

By the light of a coach lamp, Clay Reiner saw what he took from his pocket—a pair of officer's blue-and-gold shoulder straps, with the embroidered twin bars of an army captain.

"A job for you," he told his wife. "I'm useless with a needle." He turned to his son. "I thought you'd be pleased to know, Johnny," he said, looking at the astonishment and delight dawning on the youngster's face, "that this is no brevet rating—it's a real promotion! Command of a troop goes with it. I've got a long way to go yet, but I've made my start."

"Why sure, Pa!" Johnny glanced past him at Clay, and his eyes shone with joy and pride. "They know who they're dealing with. I always knew they couldn't keep *you* down!"

Sanford was assembling the Winfields' belongings, and the captain told him, "Right now we'll only take what we need for tonight. In the morning I'll send someone to carry the rest to my quarters."

The teams had been changed; the brief stop here was almost over. And now the other passengers had climbed down from the coach to meet John Winfield and say good-bye to his family. There were handshakes and last-minute embraces. Finally Clay Reiner called for their departure. The stage loaded again, with only three people now, and Reiner joined his driver on the high forward seat. The whip snapped; the horses went into their collars.

From her window, Beth Hanlon looked back and watched the Winfield family waving, until the lights of the stage station faded and Fort Union's parade ground and adobe buildings were swallowed up again in the starry immensity of the night.

Las Vegas was a grubby little Mexican pueblo, a place of morning sunlight and dust and flat-roofed adobe buildings grouped around a central plaza. On the roof of one of those buildings, in 1846, General Stephen Kearny had stood to administer to its citizens the oath of allegiance to the United States. Seventy miles of rugged mountain travel still lay ahead of the Hanlon Stage Line coach when it rolled in there, shortly after nine in the morning.

They pulled up before a native restaurant where Reiner told his passengers they could expect a good and filling breakfast. He was about to climb back to his seat to ride around to the company stable when he heard Beth Hanlon speak his name. She stood there in the winter sunlight, looking up at him with a troubled frown. After a moment's hesitation, he signaled his driver to proceed without him.

"Yes?" he asked her as the big coach rolled away.

Her head to one side, her eyes studying him, she

burst out suddenly, imploring, "What's wrong, Clay? Have I said or done something to make you angry?"

He could only stare. "How in the world could you think a thing like that?"

"*Something* must have happened. You've not spoken two words to me since we left Wootton's. I'd hate to think it was for some reason I might not even be aware of."

"But of course not," he exclaimed. "You're mistaken."

"Then why do I have this feeling you're avoiding me?"

Clay was without an answer. He looked at the hands she clasped anxiously together. High sunlight flashed a stab of brightness from the diamond on her finger; something in that helped him to steel himself. He took a slow breath. "Maybe I'm just a coward!" he blurted. "Maybe I don't find it easy to look you in the face and wonder how much you blame me for what happened to Frank Darby!"

Beth shook her head, as though not comprehending. "How in the world could I blame *you* for what happened in the pass? If Frank got—lost, it surely isn't your fault. You searched."

"And came back without him!" Reiner's voice was bleak. "And you're always going to know that I gave up, when there might still have been a chance of finding him alive. What's worse, *I'll* always know it."

"But if *I* don't blame you," she cried, "it hurts me to see you blame yourself! Someone who's been as true and good a friend, for as long as you . . ." She looked down at her hands. He watched her slowly turning the ring that now might be all she would ever have of the man she loved. Then her head lifted and a new, sober expression filled her gray eyes.

"Clay, there's something I can't help but feel I should tell you—something that happened in the pass. . . ."

"Oh?"

But whatever she might have said was interrupted. Jerry McCaig, a livery stable owner who also served as the stage company's agent in Las Vegas, sang out as he approached across the plaza dust. "Reiner! Oh, and Miss Hanlon—I didn't know you were aboard this stage."

"Is something wrong?" she asked.

"I'm afraid so. There's been some trouble."

"What kind of trouble?" Reiner wanted to know.

"Maybe you better come have a word with the night man—let him tell you about it."

Knowing that something very strange was afoot, Reiner agreed with a nod, and Beth, her own curiosity roused, went with them. They crossed the plaza to the barnlike stable, with its stock corrals in back and the big coach waiting for new teams to continue the run to Santa Fe. In McCaig's cubbyhole of an office, a man with the look of a country doctor was packing bandages and instruments into his bag. At the desk, the night stockman—a gaunt oldster named Virgil Bellman—sat with his head in his hands and a square of court plaster on his freckled and hairless scalp.

"What seems to be the matter?" Reiner demanded.

The doctor explained briefly. "He's had a bad clout on the noggin—with a gun barrel! He's only lucky it didn't kill him."

"Tell him, Virg," the stable owner grimly encouraged his man. "Just what you told me."

Bellman lifted his head as though with an effort. Eyes dulled with the pain of a massive headache, the hostler got his story out. "It was near two in the morning, or thereabouts," he said, "when I heard something bothering the horses in the corral. I took a lantern and went out there— thought a varmint might be after them. I was right! It was a two-legged varmint! He jumped me and laid me out cold." He clutched his head and groaned. "God! It *hurts*!"

"We found him about half an hour ago," McCaig supplied, "lying in the brush out behind the corrals. And there's a horse missing."

"A stage company horse?" Reiner wanted to know.

"No, no. One of my rent string—good riding stock.

166

The fellow apparently had his own saddle and gear. I hunted around and found the animal he'd switched from, looking hard ridden and played out."

"Then I can't see how this has anything directly to do with the Hanlon Stage Line."

McCaig and the hostler and the doctor shared a look. The liveryman said gruffly, "Go on, Virg. Give him the rest of it."

Bellman's gaunt shoulders lifted on a shaky breath. He continued in the same dull voice. "Like I said, I had a lantern. It give me a good look at the sonofabitch just before he hit me. Fact is, I was too surprised even to duck—because I *knew* him! It was a fellow that works for your boss. Man named Darby. . . ."

Beth Hanlon gasped. Reiner just stared, then said, "You're mistaken. It couldn't have been!"

"Don't tell *me* it couldn't have been!" the injured man flared at him. "I guess I know Frank Darby when I see him—and he knows I do! Hell, I called out his name just before he let me have the gun barrel. Doc says there ain't any question he was aiming to kill me!" And the doctor's nod confirmed this as he snapped the catch of his bag.

Stunned, Clay turned to look at Beth. Her face was completely drained of color. The look she gave him was one of bewilderment and disbelief. "What is he saying?" she exclaimed in a small voice. "It's impossible!"

"Of course it is!"

But the old man's certainty was unshakable. McCaig added, "The tracks point toward the Santa Fe road; looks like that's where he was headed. Oh—one more thing. I found Virg with his pockets emptied and turned inside out—like some ordinary thief done it. Only, there wasn't any sign of anybody around but Darby!"

That was when Reiner felt Beth's hand slip into his own. Her fingers were cold and trembling; they tugged at him, and he heard the urgency as she said, in a tremulous murmur, "Clay! I have to talk to you!"

He made an excuse, and a moment later they were outside with a ground wind across the plaza blowing gritty dust against them. Facing Beth and the stricken look she showed him, Reiner said quickly, "Now, you're not to let this upset you, hear me? The whole thing is going to turn out to be some obvious mistake. We both know it."

"I wish I *did* know it, for certain," she said almost inaudibly.

"What in the world do you mean?"

It came spilling out. "Just this—ever since we ran into him at Bent's Fort, I've been wondering more and more about Frank. He acted so strangely! He begged me to get on the eastbound coach, right then and there, and go away with him. He said he'd had a fight with Pa over something and quit his job, and he couldn't return to Santa Fe. He didn't even try to explain. I talked him into letting me do what I could to straighten matters out, but he didn't like it at all. And then he got an idea that we should be married when we got to Trinidad. From something in the way he talked and acted, I had to tell him *no*! Clay, I can't explain. I just had a feeling that it was—all *wrong*!"

When she stopped for breath, Reiner broke in. "I can't see that this has any bearing on what the old man in there just told us. Whatever frame of mind he might have been in, we still left Frank Darby up at Raton Pass. Or are you trying somehow to say we're wrong about that? That somehow or other he got here *ahead* of us—that he was the one who stole a horse from the corral last night and tried to kill Virg Bellman?"

"Just as poor Ned Archer was killed, remember?" she pointed out. "Just exactly like that—even to emptying his pockets! And Frank was with Ned that evening in Trinidad; he admitted it! It's terrible even to imagine that Frank could be a killer, but—" She steeled herself to finish. "There was something I started to tell you, a few minutes ago. During the shooting at the pass, Frank tried to kill *you*! I saw him. He said he mistook you for one of the deserters—and I wanted to believe it. But now I'm convinced he was lying. I think he must have hated you, Clay—or was afraid of you. Maybe both!"

For a long moment, Reiner could only stare at her. All too vividly he was remembering a bullet that had narrowly missed him—a bullet he was sure had been fired from the beleaguered stagecoach. When he spoke, it was to say heavily, "I'd hate to think bad of Frank Darby. It's all too easy to do, when you're jealous of someone."

"*You?* Jealous of Frank?" Beth's eyes widened. "But why in the world—?" And then she must have read the answer that his look unintentionally revealed. Her expression altered; her gray eyes appeared to darken with astonishment. "You don't mean—?"

"What if I do?" he snapped, angry with himself for having let her glimpse his most deeply hidden secret. "That's *my* problem—only right now it makes it hard for me to keep an open mind. I honestly don't know what to think about all this. Yet it could mean there's an outside chance Darby is somewhere out in front of us right now— headed for Santa Fe. And we don't even know why!"

"You don't suppose . . ." Suddenly her hand was on his arm, tightening urgently. "All at once I have such a terrible feeling! I'm remembering how he looked when he was telling me about his trouble with Pa. And, Clay—it *scares* me!"

Her very real concern settled his own mind. He nodded and placed his hand on hers. "All right, Beth." He called into the stable then. "McCaig! Will you pick me out a horse that has some bottom to him, and get him saddled up? I need him—quick!" To Beth, he explained, "You and your mother and uncle should make out fine now, without me. With the start Darby has, there's only one way in the world I got a prayer of catching up with him."

She nodded quick agreement—and then turned and added a call of her own: "Make that two horses, Mr. McCaig. . . . I'm going with you," she told Reiner.

"Oh, no you're not!"

Her head came up and she faced him, sudden color flaming in her cheeks. "Don't try to give me orders, Clay Reiner!" she exclaimed imperiously. And in that instant, her look and manner reminded him so much of tough old Tom Hanlon that Reiner almost grinned in surprise and admiration. But then her mouth trembled and her eyes shone as she added, in an entirely different tone, "Oh, please! You can't ask me to poke along in that coach the rest of the way—wondering all the time what might be happening, and unable to do anything about it! Clay, I'll go crazy!" Her hand tightened as she pleaded. "I won't be any trouble at all, or hold you back. I was all but raised on a horse—you know that. I can ride every bit as well as you can!"

He knew he should refuse, and yet he could understand how desperately serious she was. "We got a long ride ahead," he pointed out. "Seventy miles or so. It won't be any picnic. And what am I to tell your mother? The last thing we want is to give her any call for worry about you—or about Tom."

Beth considered that, then shook her head in quick resolution. "No. You see to the horses; *I'll* tell Mother."

"Tell her what?" he demanded suspiciously when he detected a familiar and roguish glint in her eye.

"Why, the truth mostly—that you decided you had business in town that wouldn't wait on the coach any longer. And I was so cramped from being cooped up that when you suggested I ride along and keep you company, I couldn't resist the invitation."

"I don't remember any invitation," he smiled.

"Don't be technical," she chided him, then hurried off to find her mother.

Chapter 15

The New Mexico extension of the Rocky Mountains—
the Sangre de Cristos—formed a last formidable barrier.
Because of it the Santa Fe road had to take a looping
detour to the south and then northwest, through a rugged
land of mesas and tilted hogbacks, of sandstone and shales
laid down by prehistoric seas. It was an old land, dotted
with ruins and with scattered Mexican settlements, rich in
the lore of the Pueblo Indians and of the old Spaniards
who had been the first Europeans to disrupt an ancient
way of life. Only after it had crossed the Pecos River and
made the long ascent of Glorieta Pass could the ancient
highway push directly on to Santa Fe. Someone had said
the barren red hills it traversed, with their spotting of
piñon pine, looked just like hams studded with cloves and
ready for the oven.

Though Beth was determined not to be any hindrance,
Clay Reiner held back, not pushing as hard as he likely
would have had he been alone. Beth was a good horse-
woman, trained from childhood and as able as most men.
Still, she had had a long and dangerous journey, and he
didn't need to be told how fine-strung it must have left
her—probably nearer nervous and physical exhaustion than
she herself could realize. For his part, he had to admit
that he was glad of Beth's company, even though they
rode mostly in silence; the name of Darby no longer
passed between them, though he was undoubtedly prominent in the thoughts of each.

At every likely point along the way, Reiner inquired about him, but no one had seen a man of that description. He might be staying carefully out of sight, or they might be chasing a man who had never come this way at all. But it never once occurred to Reiner that he should give up pursuit.

Beth seemed to have a number of things on her mind, as well. Once, when they stopped to rest their horses and share a cold meal from food she had foreseen to bring along from the restaurant at Las Vegas, Reiner found her regarding him with a thoughtful look. He was finally driven to ask, "Is something bothering you?"

The question caught her off guard. She hesitated before reluctantly answering, "This morning you said something I didn't fully understand. About jealousy. . . ."

"Oh." He dropped his eyes to the pipe he was in the process of filling from his tobacco pouch. "It's an easy enough word," he said gruffly. "What's hard to understand about it?"

"Did you seriously mean you were jealous of Frank Darby—on *my* account? Is that what you were trying to tell me, Clay?"

His fingers tightened on the bowl of the pipe. Still not looking at her, he replied, "You shouldn't hold it against me. I was pretty much worked up at the moment. It just came out."

"Then you *didn't* mean it."

He raised his eyes to meet her serious and questioning look. "I didn't mean you should ever know," he said finally. "Beth, you and I have been friends a long time. There's nothing else in my life I count higher than that friendship. But I've never fooled myself into thinking it would go beyond that. The day we left Hays City, I heard your uncle Harris call me a roughneck—and it's one thing he's said that I couldn't give him an argument about! Because if I thought different—if I supposed, for a minute, I was anywhere near good enough—d'you think I'd have stood by and watched while Frank Darby, or anyone else, came along and put an uncontested claim on some-one I cared for that much?"

"But Clay!" Beth shook her head, her eyes darkened with feeling. "I—I just don't know what to say! I never dreamed. . . . You never once let on." Involuntarily her hand moved toward him. And then, as the sun caught a facet of the diamond on her finger, they both were left staring at the ring—and it was like a warning barrier raised between them.

There was suddenly nothing to say. Abruptly, Clay got up from the rock where they had been sitting. Stowing away his pipe, he began to gather up the remains of their brief meal. "We better be getting along," he told her stiffly.

He would have helped Beth to mount, but she found the stirrup and swung astride unaided. In moments, they were riding again through the crisp winter day, with the sun dipping toward the mountains ahead of them. And they rode in deep silence, starting the climb toward Glorieta Pass.

Dusk was settling as they came wearily through the first outlying scatter of adobe hovels and so into the cramped and twisted streets of Santa Fe. Smells of cooking, of piñon smoke and dust and animal dung, rode the strength-ening air currents of coming night. Lamplight glowed behind narrow, barred windows of houses that turned blank and expressionless faces to the world. Overhead, stars were glimmering into sight against a sky turned steel-gray, above distant mountains like black cutouts on the horizon.

Clay and Beth dismounted in front of her father's house, easing muscles punished by the ache and stiffness of hours of riding. They tied their horses to an iron ring set into the whitewashed wall. The big wooden door would be barred from within; Reiner worked the bell pull and they waited, until the door was cracked open cautiously and then flung wide as Serafina rushed out to greet her mistress with cries of pleasure, hugging Beth to her ample bosom.

The housekeeper had been almost a mother to Beth, particularly since her parents' separation. Now, as Serafina ushered the new arrivals into the Hanlon home, the two women kept up an excited exchange in Spanish, a second language for Beth. The mood of homecoming was interrupted on a sober note, however, when the young woman asked about her father.

"The señor sleeps just now," she was told. "I looked in on him only a moment ago. Today he has had much pain, and he took laudanum hoping to be given a restful night."

"I hope he gets it," Clay replied, also in Spanish. When the woman had given further details that corroborated the earlier reports Reiner had received, he continued, "I was hoping for a word with Tom, but it looks like that's out of the question for the time being. Right now I'm looking for Frank Darby. Have you seen him?"

Serafina shook her head; the disdainful expression on her dark face made no secret of her feelings about the man, even if he was her beloved Beth's fiancé. "I have not seen that one," she said coldly. "Not since—let me think— it would be last Tuesday evening. He was in the señor's bedroom and they were quarrelling."

"Quarrelling?" Reiner echoed. "What about, do you know?"

The woman shrugged. "It is not my business to know. But they were so loud I became frightened at what might happen, and I went running in one time to find out what was wrong."

"And?"

"All I know is that the señor and Darby were both very angry. I heard something about prison, and some money that had been taken, and that Señor Darby was to leave next morning for Denver to bring the money back. Of course, I did not hear very much."

Serafina, Reiner thought shrewdly, could be counted on to miss very little of what went on in the Hanlon house, especially if it had serious meaning for any precious member of that family. A sudden thought made him ask, "Was Ned Archer in the room?"

She shook her head. "It is almost an hour after the man Darby left that Señor Archer arrived. I do not know what he and the señor have talked about, though I may have heard—just happened to overhear, you understand—that he would also be leaving on the stagecoach next day, for Denver."

"I see. . . ."

Beth was staring at him, trying to read his thoughtful frown. She laid a hand on his arm. "Clay! What can this all mean?"

"I could make a guess," he answered bleakly, "but I'd rather wait and get it directly from your father. For now, I'm going to get rid of those horses and then start looking for Frank Darby. If he's actually here in Santa Fe, *somebody* ought to have seen him."

"And what if you find him?"

"Far as I'm concerned, I just want to ask the man some questions," Reiner said flatly. "Anything else will be up to Darby. . . ."

Being home again, in the familiar surroundings of her father's house, seemed to nullify and make unreal the jumble of these past days and nights—the ordeal of travel and the dangers she had survived. Beth had not realized how tired she really was until all action suddenly came to a halt—until, at last, she stood beside her father's bed and looked at his sleeping face. A low-burning lamp showed her the change in him: the hollowing of his cheeks that turned him into something he had never seemed before— an old man. Even in drugged sleep, Tom Hanlon's fea-

tures showed lines of suffering that touched her heart with
love and pity.

Her father had been a hard man, but never less than
gentle with her. If he drove the men who worked for him,
he had always driven himself harder. "Oh, Pa!" Beth said
aloud, as she gently smoothed back the thinning hair from
his forehead. "The unhappiness you've given to others—
and to yourself! I'm sure you didn't *mean* to drive Mother
away. But couldn't you say even a word to admit you
needed her? Did you think it was a sign of weakness? I
wonder if this has taught you that no one is as strong as all
that. . . ."

Serafina called her to supper, which she served on
the massive table in the low-ceilinged dining room. Beth
hadn't had such a meal in all the days since she and her
mother started west, yet she was almost too weary to
enjoy it. As she was finishing, Serafina came to report that
her bed was made up and waiting. But Beth shook her
head.

"I just don't know," she sighed. "Have you ever been
so tired you couldn't sleep? I think I'll go in and sit with
Pa awhile, on the chance he might wake up." The woman
at once became anxious and had to be assured there was
nothing wrong other than simple fatigue, compounded by
weeks of worry and the stress of a hectic journey.

Beth took a book with her into the sickroom, but
decided she wasn't up to reading. It was more relaxing
and pleasant to sit in a comfortable chair in a shadowed
corner, where the dim glow of the bedside lamp failed to
reach. She sat and listened to the ticking of a clock, to the
small noises of the old house, and to her father's steady
breathing. Her head seemed to grow heavy, the world
withdrew to a great distance. She never knew when her
eyes closed and she slept, or how much time had passed
when something woke her.

Still in a fog of sleep, she saw a man standing by the
bed and thought at first she must be dreaming. But the

figure failed to vanish, and slowly it dawned on her the man was real enough. All at once fully awake, she started to rise. The book forgotten in her lap slipped to the floor; the man's head jerked up as he heard. He turned, and it was Frank Darby.

He was the first to recover. "Beth!" he exclaimed. "What in the world are you doing here?"

"I could ask you the same!" she countered, on her feet now. She had never seen him like this—unshaven, his clothing travel-stained, and with a narrow, watchful expression on his face. Then she noticed what was in his hands as he hovered over the bed—and an icy finger seemed to touch her. "That pillow! What were you going to do with it?"

He looked at it, then shrugged and tossed it on the bed. "Just rearranging things. Trying to make him more comfortable."

"I think he's perfectly comfortable," Beth said coldly. "He's taken laudanum. He's dead to the world!"

They regarded one another, a wall of unvoiced suspicion between them. Presently Beth asked, "How did you get into the house? I don't think Serafina would have let you in."

"Probably not; she doesn't like me. But there are always other ways." He added, "I certainly didn't expect to find *you*. When did the stage get in, anyway?"

"It hasn't yet. Clay and I left it at Vegas and rode on ahead."

"Clay and you?" He looked around quickly.

"He's not here," Beth told him. "Don't worry—there's only the two of us." All at once she felt herself beginning to tremble with anger and impatience over this endless sparring. She heard herself say, "Why do we stand here talking in circles, Frank? Why don't we both say what we're really thinking?"

"I'm not sure I know what you mean." His tone was mild, but his look was probing and careful.

"I mean, that I want to know what happened up at the pass. All of a sudden you just weren't there. Clay and the others hunted and hunted, but they couldn't find a trace. In the end we had no choice but to come on without you. And now, without warning—here you are in Santa Fe! Don't you think that needs some explaining?"

He hesitated only a moment. "But the answer's quite simple," he told her smoothly. "In the storm and the fighting, I became confused and found myself lost. I never knew anyone was looking for me. With night coming on, I'll admit I began to think I could die out there! Then just by chance, I stumbled across a saddled horse—it must have belonged to one of those men who hit the stage. At any rate, it saved my life. But by the time I found my way back to the road, the stage was already gone, and everything was dark at Wootton's. I knew you'd be concerned about me, so I just let myself through the gate and came on, trying to catch up. I still don't see why I never did."

"It's because we stayed that night at Wootton's," she explained. "The boy was badly hurt, and Clay decided not to go on until morning."

"And by that time I was already miles ahead of you. There's no way I could have guessed *that*. I would never have imagined that fellow Reiner risking a schedule, for any reason!" He shrugged. "Well, anyway, I kept pushing until it finally dawned on me that we must have missed connections somehow. After that it was too late to do anything but go on." He added anxiously, "Darling, if there's anything else that's bothering you, please say so! I can't bear to have misunderstandings between us!"

She hesitated. He was so earnest and forthcoming that, for a moment, her old feeling for the man almost overcame her doubts of him. Had he taken her into his arms just then, he might actually have won. But he only looked at her, and Beth slowly shook her head.

She told him quietly, "I'd like to hear some more about the fight you had with Pa. Your quarrel wasn't entirely about me. Why don't you admit it had to do with the money you stole?"

The change in him was startling. He looked for an instant as though she had struck him. Then his mouth settled. He jerked around to stare at the old man on the bed. "So he *talked!*" he exclaimed in a tone of sudden violence. "Damn the old bastard, he's told you!"

Anger carried her past a terrible moment of faintness. She said coldly, "Don't talk like that about my pa!" It was enough to warn him of his damaging error, and he tried quickly to amend it.

"Darling, I'm sorry—I really am! I know how much you love him. But—I thought you also loved *me*. Would you stand by and let him send me to prison, all because of a bad piece of business judgment? Because that's all it was," he insisted. "In a way I'm really glad that you found out about it. I just saw a chance to get the money I needed for you—for *us*. Naturally I was going to pay back what I took, and I told him so. You can't possibly not believe that!"

This time he did try to reach for her, but he missed his timing. Beth moved away a step, evading him, and when she replied, her words were heavy with accusation and bitter knowledge. "But you didn't go to Denver and get the money, as you promised Pa. When I met you at Bent's Fort, you were on your way out of this country. You tried to talk me into going with you, so you would never have to face him again. The fact is—you were *running!*" Her eyes burned through him. "No, I don't believe you," she went on, not waiting for him to answer. "Pa didn't either. He sent poor Ned Archer along to make sure you *did* go to Denver—and so Ned had to be put out of the way. Just as I believe you were trying to do to Clay Reiner during that fight at the pass!"

"Beth, be careful. You're accusing me of murder!"

She plunged ahead, intent now on getting everything into the open. "That's still not all the story! The fight gave you what you thought would be a perfect alibi. You let us believe you were lost in the storm, while you rushed down here ahead of us and broke into the house intending to kill Pa in his sleep—smother him with that pillow and leave nobody to accuse you of anything when you finally showed up alive and well! But your scheme never would have worked, even if I hadn't been here to stop you. Because there's Bellman—the man you left for dead at that corral in Las Vegas. He didn't die, Frank! He's alive—and he's identified you. So you see, you have no alibi. Instead, you've put yourself in deep trouble!"

She had to stop then and try to steady her breathing and the furious pounding of her heart. Frank Darby's face was a mask that hid whatever feelings were roiling behind it. His voice, when he spoke, seemed unnaturally quiet—as though he were holding it under an immense effort of control. "Are you finished now?"

"Yes!" she managed to get out, then instantly corrected herself. "No—not quite. Frank, if I've made a mistake, I'm sorry. But I don't really think I have. Either way, it's obvious whatever there was between us is finished. You'll be wanting this back. . . ." She was surprised not to feel anything at all as she drew off the engagement ring and held it out to him. He only stared at it. Then suddenly, with a curse, he struck it from her fingers.

"So it's over, is it?" he gritted in a voice she had never heard before. "Just like that! You know, of course, the whole thing is your fault!"

"*My* fault?" She couldn't believe her ears.

"If you'd only done what I asked and gone away with me, this could all have been behind us now. Even at Trinidad there was still time. You could have agreed to marry me. Then Tom Hanlon would never have dared press charges, not against your husband—his son-in-law. But no! Damn you, you've turned out to be every bit as muleheaded as the old man ever was!"

180

He cursed her again, savagely, and the flat of his hand swept across her cheek. Beth cried out and would have fallen, but Darby's left hand seized her and held her up, pulling her close so that she looked, dazed, directly into his angry, blazing stare.

"And to think I wasted a year of my life on you!" He almost whispered it, in a tone of pure contempt. "Thinking you were different—thinking you were worth sacrificing for. You little bitch!" And he slapped her again.

This time her knees gave way and she fell, her limp weight pulling free of his grip as she went down onto the hard tiles of the floor. Through the ringing that filled her head, she imagined she heard a voice loudly shouting Frank Darby's name. She tried to push herself up. Crouching there, she saw Darby looming above her. He turned quickly to face the doorway—and Beth saw Clay Reiner come bursting in.

The action that followed was almost too swift for her to grasp, dazed as she was by Darby's numbing blow. She saw Darby stab a fist at Reiner, only to have it blocked and deflected against a forearm. And then Reiner struck, and Darby's head jerked hard upon his shoulders. Frank Darby was driven backward, stumbling. He knocked a table over with a crash. He caught his footing, only to receive another blow that put him sprawling on his back, his face a bloody mess from the nose that had been mashed flat. He seemed, groggily, to remember the gun behind his waistband; Beth tried to gasp a warning as she saw him fumble it out and raise it against his enemy, but no sound came from her.

Clay Reiner was not to be caught off guard. He had a weapon in his holster, but he made no move toward it. Instead, he simply took a stride forward. His boot swung, struck Darby on the side of the head, and the gun went spinning from his hand, to strike against the wall. Then Darby fell back, unconscious. Reiner stood over the man long enough to make sure there was no fight left in him.

After that, he hurried to Beth and sank to his knees. His arms went around her, and she clutched and clung to him. All at once her control gave way. She pressed her face against him and began to cry.

"Beth!" he exclaimed, over and over. "My darling!" And neither seemed to notice he was using a word he had never spoken to her before. "Tell me! Did he—?"

"I'm all right." She pulled back, angry at her own tears. She rubbed her hands across her cheeks to dry them, and winced as she found a tender place. "He *hit* me!" she gasped, still not quite ready to believe it. "Twice. . . ."

"I wish I'd known!" Clay said in a tone that startled her so much that she looked at him—and she saw the white anger in his face. "I'd have pounded him harder! Any man who'd lay a hand on *you!* . . ."

"It's all right," she said quickly. "Let it go—he's not worth it."

Somewhere in the house, a clock was striking midnight. Clay explained briefly, "I hunted all over town and couldn't locate anyone who'd ever seen the man. So I finally gave it up and came back. . . . Oh, God! Not a minute too soon!"

She lifted a hand to touch his face, close to her own: a strong face, one long familiar and—she suddenly realized—infinitely dear to her. It seemed incredible that she could have mistaken her feeling for him, or ever thought herself in love with any other man. Certainly it was the most natural thing in the world, then, that they should kiss, and then kiss a second time—and that every other thing should be forgotten until the approaching sound of voices and footsteps brought them back to an awareness of the rest of the world.

Clay was just helping Beth to her feet when her uncle came rushing in, with Mary Hanlon and Serafina close behind—the Santa Fe stage had finally arrived! Harris McRae halted in midstride. "What in the world—?" He stared at the overturned table, caught sight of the man sprawled on the floor, his head bruised and bloody. "Darby! He couldn't be *here*! What's been going on, anyway?"

Beth gathered her strength to answer, but Reiner said quickly, "It's a long story, McRae; time enough for it later. Just give me a hand and let's put this man on his feet. The law's going to want something to do with him. . . ."

Mary went directly to her husband's bedside. She lifted one of Tom's limp hands in both of hers and bent to kiss his cheek; he stirred to her touch, but gave no sign of waking. Mary's cheeks shone with tears as her daughter walked over to join her. "I was so wrong to leave him, Beth!" she exclaimed. "All because my pride was hurt!"

Beth placed an arm around her waist. "We've all made our share of mistakes, Mother," she pointed out. "You, and Pa—and me! But at least it doesn't have to be too late. . . ."

Frank Darby was on his feet and being led, bleeding and groggy, to the door. The sight of him made Beth shudder as she realized what all too easily might have been.

But then he was forgotten, as Beth looked with the eyes of love at strong and gentle Clay Reiner. *Yes!* she thought. *Thank heaven it isn't too late!*

★ WAGONS WEST ★

A series of unforgettable books that trace the lives of a dauntless band of pioneering men, women and children as they brave the hazards of an untamed land in their trek across America. This legendary caravan of people forge a new link in the wilderness. They are Americans from the North and the South, alongside immigrants, Blacks, and Indians, who wage fierce daily battle for survival in this uncompromising journey—each to their private destinies as they fulfill their greatest dreams.

DON'T MISS A SINGLE VOLUME IN AMERICA'S
#1 SERIES—WAGONS WEST!

( ) *INDEPENDENCE! BOOK I (22808-0 * $3.50)*
( ) *NEBRASKA! BOOK II (22784-X * $3.50)*
( ) *WYOMING! BOOK III (23177-4 * $3.50)*
( ) *OREGON! BOOK IV (22568-5 * $3.50)*
( ) *TEXAS! BOOK V (23168-5 * $3.50)*
( ) *CALIFORNIA! BOOK VI (23381-5 * $3.50)*
( ) *COLORADO! BOOK VII (23405-6 * $3.50)*
( ) *NEVADA! BOOK VIII (20174-3 * $3.50)*
( ) *WASHINGTON! BOOK IX (20919-1 * $3.50)*
( ) *MONTANA! BOOK X (22925-7 * $3.95)*
( ) *DAKOTA! BOOK XI (23572-9 $3.95)*

Buy these books at your local bookstore or use this handy coupon for ordering: